A Going Concern

Catherine Aird served as Chairman of the Crime Writers' Association from 1990 to 1991 and is the author of some fifteen crime novels. She has also written a *son et lumière* and has edited a number of parish histories. Though she has lived in east Kent for many years, she was brought up in Huddersfield.

In October 1992 she was the first recipient of the CWA/Hertfordshire Libraries Golden Handcuffs Award for her outstanding contribution to detective fiction.

A Going Concern

Catherine Aird

PAN BOOKS
IN ASSOCIATION WITH MACMILLAN LONDON

First published 1993 by Macmillan London Limited

This edition published 1994 by Pan Books Limited
a division of Pan Macmillan Publishers Limited
Cavaye Place, London SW10 9PG
and Basingstoke
in association with Macmillan London Limited

Associated companies throughout the world

ISBN 0 330 33038 1

1 3 5 7 9 8 6 4 2

A CIP catalogue record for this book is available from
the British Library

Phototypeset by Intype, London
Printed and bound in Great Britain by
Cox & Wyman Ltd, Reading, Berkshire

For Louis and Joan
with affection

The chapter headings comprise
'The Burial of the Linnet'
by Mrs Ewing.

ONE

Found in the garden dead in his beauty –

The undertakers had been very helpful.

No, she thought immediately to herself, that wasn't putting it anything like strongly enough. She promptly rephrased the sentiment in her mind.

Messrs J. Morton and Sons, Funeral Furnishers, of Nethergate Street, Berebury, couldn't in the circumstances – the rather special circumstances – possibly have done more than they had done.

Even that, she felt on consideration, wasn't quite stating the true position really fairly.

Amelia, no dissembler, braced her shoulders and for the very first time she admitted the whole truth to herself: which was that without young Tod Morton's help she wouldn't even have known where to begin to arrange this particular funeral.

And here she was, only a week after Tod Morton had first spoken to her, following her Great-Aunt Octavia's coffin up the path towards the church of St Hilary in the small village of Great Primer in the county of Calleshire after the manner born.

It was after the manor born, too, as it happened. Great-Aunt Octavia's cortège had set off only a very short time before from her home – the Grange at Great Primer – which was near enough to the church for the tardiest worshipper: a quick walker might even have waited for the minute bell before starting out.

Amelia had followed in the first car behind the hearse, which was a clear sign to everyone else there of her position.

The police had not been at all happy about this, earnestly counselling a rather lower profile, but in this respect Amelia had been adamant. Chief mourner at the funeral she was and in the place of chief mourner at the funeral she would be.

And now Tod Morton, wearing a black suit with striped trousers, black gloves and top hat in hand, was standing discreetly at her elbow the while and indicating to her what to do as if she had known him all her life instead of only seven days.

The last seven days.

It had all begun with a death.

Funerals usually did, thought Amelia grimly, following Tod Morton's unobtrusive directions with child-like obedience. As the coffin was carried through the lich-gate she found it quite difficult to believe that this time last week she'd been in the middle of a carefree holiday abroad.

In fact she had been vacationing in France when the strange message about her Great-Aunt Octavia's death had reached her. She and three of her friends had been renting a *gîte* for the month of August. They'd all shared school and then college and a certain indefinable nostalgia had been keeping them together still for one last holiday before they were severally claimed by life and work.

It had been Mary-Louise who had actually picked up the telephone receiver when the instrument gave its unfamiliar Gallic trill. And she had been expecting nothing more earth-shattering than her mother ringing from home with her examination results. Until that moment young Mary-Louise hadn't thought that anything more earth-shattering existed than examination results.

'It's for you, Milly.' Mary-Louise had looked quite

distressed. 'It's an undertaker ringing from England.'

In the space of time that it had taken Amelia to cross the room to the telephone she knew beyond doubt that it couldn't have been her father who had died. If it had been, then Phoebe – dear Phoebe – would have told her so herself even if she had had to down tools and come out to Dordogne in person to do so. And yet, thought Amelia, very puzzled, it was only her stepmother Phoebe who had the telephone number of their holiday cottage near Montpazier.

'Is that Miss Kennerley?' Tod Morton had asked.

'Yes,' said Amelia cautiously.

'Dr Plantin told me how to get in touch with you.'

Amelia had been even more reassured. Come hell or high water, Phoebe Plantin would never have delegated the breaking of really bad news to anyone else, but least of all to an unknown undertaker telephoning from another country. That, at least, confirmed her view that nothing terrible had happened to her father.

'What about?' she had said then to Tod Morton. He could hardly be ringing about her own mother's grave. Nothing urgent happened to graves already twelve years old. She realized at once that her question must have sounded inept and ungrammatical and she had amended it before the voice at the other end could answer. Ironically, two weeks spent concentrating on the French language had already done something for her English. 'Has somebody died?'

'A Mrs Octavia Garamond of the Grange, Great Primer . . .'

'My great-aunt . . .' Amelia knitted her brow. 'That is, I think that's who she is.'

'Yes, miss. That's what Dr Phoebe said.'

So her stepmother was 'Dr Phoebe' to Tod Morton as she was to half the population of the market town of Berebury.

'I'm afraid, miss,' he went on, 'that she died last night.'

'Well,' said Amelia, 'she was very old. She must have been.' Mrs Octavia Garamond had been one of her dead mother's aunts – or, to be more precise – the widow of her late mother's uncle William.

'Yes, miss,' said Tod Morton. 'So I understand . . .'

'It's very kind of you to have rung me.' Amelia cast about in her mind for what to say next, and asked: 'When is the funeral to be?'

Her father, she decided, must be off on one of his famous field trips. If he had been at home in Calleshire he would undoubtedly have dealt with the matter himself, and perhaps even gone out into the country to the village of Great Primer for the funeral, snatching time from his desk of course with the greatest reluctance. After all, her father probably even remembered Great-Aunt Octavia from the old days when he – and she – had both been members of the extended Garamond family: it would have been easier for him anyway. Her father was an anthropologist and a great authority on extended families . . .

'That's really for you to say, miss,' replied the voice at the other end of the telephone.

'Me?' Amelia very nearly said, 'What am I to Hecuba, that I should weep for her?' but she didn't. This was no time for William Shakespeare and the Prince of Denmark. She said instead, rather lamely, 'Why me?'

'I understand,' said Tod Morton, clearing his throat, 'from the late Mrs Garamond's solicitors, Messrs Puckle, Puckle, and Nunnery, that you are her executrix.'

Amelia Kennerley very nearly said 'Me?' again from sheer surprise. She swallowed rapidly and said 'Me and who else?' instead, sounding, if she had known it, rather like the comedian Rob Wilton in his famous sketch about having to win the war single-handed.

'Sole executrix,' said the voice at the other end of the continental telephone.

4

'What! . . . Oh, I'm sorry,' Amelia apologized automatically, her mind in a total whirl: she thought she could
just remember having seen her great-aunt. Only just,
though. It must have been when she had been a very
little girl indeed but it was true that she could conjure up
in her mind's eye an unfocused picture of a strange house
where she had held on to her mother's hand rather tightly
while an unknown old lady (when you are small, all
grown-ups are old) spoke to her. Amelia pulled herself
together and said: 'I mean, did she leave any instructions
about her funeral?'

She knew that people did this because her own mother
had apparently said long before she died that she wanted
to be buried by the bell tower at Almstone. She'd always
liked the sound of church bells . . .

'I understand from Mr Puckle – that's Mr James Puckle
– young Mr James, that is, not his uncle or grandfather
– that Mrs Garamond had indicated in her testamentary
dispositions a wish for burial . . .'

Amelia's mind had gone off at a complete tangent,
trying to work out however many Puckles there must be
in the firm. The old saw about thrift came into her mind:
'Many a mickle makes a muckle . . .' Could it be a case
of many a client making a Puckle?

Tod Morton was still speaking. 'In the churchyard of
St Hilary's at Great Primer beside the graves of her husband and daughter.'

It was beginning to come back to Amelia now. She
could remember hearing that her late mother had had a
cousin who had also died young. Dying young seemed to
have been a characteristic of her mother's family . . .

'Well, then . . .' she had said to Tod Morton.

He coughed delicately. 'I understand from Mr Puckle
that as sole executrix the actual decision is yours. Executors and next-of-kin can over-rule the expressed wishes
of the deceased.'

'I shouldn't dream of doing any such thing,' rejoined Amelia crisply.

'That's what I thought,' said Tod Morton at once, 'so I've spoken to the rector of Great Primer about having the Garamond family grave opened up.'

'Good.'

'And also made provisional arrangements for a funeral service to be held at St Hilary's parish church at Great Primer on Friday next, that is, today week.'

'Good,' said Amelia again.

'Subject to your approval.'

'You have it,' said Amelia. She still felt quite bemused. 'Tell me, Mr . . . er . . .?'

'Morton, miss,' the voice had said helpfully. 'Tod Morton.'

'Tell me, Mr Morton, did Mr Puckle – Mr James Puckle – say . . . I mean, is it known . . . why Mrs Garamond made me her sole executrix?' It seemed to Amelia such a very long time ago that her mother had presented her to someone who even then had seemed as old as the hills: and even that memory was more than a little uncertain now.

Of one thing, though, she was sure. It had been before she, Amelia, had become known within the family as 'poor Helena's girl'.

'I couldn't say, miss, I'm sure,' said Tod Morton. 'All I know is that her doctor told the solicitors that Mrs Garamond had died and they told me.'

Amelia Kennerley suppressed a strong desire to add 'and they went and told the sexton and the sexton toll'd the bell'. Quotations from parodies of 'Who Killed Cock Robin?' were even less appropriate to the situation than those from *Hamlet*.

'And I told Mr Fournier . . . that's Mr Edwin Fournier,' continued Tod Morton, who not unnaturally had no means of knowing what was going through her mind.

6

'Mr Fournier?'

'He's the parson out at Great Primer,' replied Tod. 'Sorry, miss, I didn't quite catch what you said then.'

A feeling akin to hysteria had almost overwhelmed Amelia. She struggled for the right words. She must say something that had no connection at all with Cock Robin. 'What did Mr Fournier say?'

There was a pause at the end of the continental telephone: a longer pause than she had expected. It couldn't be surely – could it – that Tod Morton – he sounded quite young over the telephone – was also trying hard not to say:

Who'll bear the pall?
We, said the wren,
Both the cock and the hen,
We'll bear the pall?

It wasn't.

When he did reply to her, Tod Morton seemed to be choosing his words with unusual care and he reported something quite unexpected. He said: 'When I told Mr Fournier that old Mrs Garamond up at the Grange had died and could he take the funeral service . . .'

'Yes?'

'He said to me, miss, that it was both his Christian duty and his legal duty under English canon law to conduct Mrs Garamond's funeral in a seemly and Christian fashion with a service from the Prayer Book . . .'

Even Amelia, inexperienced in these matters as she was, thought this an unusual reaction by a man in Holy Orders to the news of the death of one of his parishioners.

'And,' continued Tod, 'he said seeing as he was therefore bound to do so, do it he would.' The undertaker sniffed. 'If you were to ask me, miss, it sounded to me a bit as if he was miffed about something and that he'd sort

7

of rehearsed what he was going to say against the time, like.'

Somewhere at the back of Amelia's mind she thought she remembered that burying the dead was one of the Contrary Virtues; the Contrary Virtues had been a puzzle to her at Sunday School until she got it into her head at last that they were called 'Contrary' because they were the opposite of the Capital Sins and not just plain awkward like in 'Mary, Mary, quite contrary'.

'Mr Fournier . . .' Tod Morton began a second time.

No, she thought again, burying the dead wasn't one of the Contrary Virtues after all. Surely Burying the Dead was one of the Seven Corporal Works of Mercy? Like Harbouring the Harbourless . . .

'Mr Fournier did say . . .' persisted the undertaker.

And, thought Amelia, surely the rector couldn't say he wouldn't bury her great-aunt, could he? Anyway, evidently he hadn't because Tod Morton was saying something else now . . .

'Mr Fournier,' Tod Morton had finally succeeded in getting her full attention, 'did say to me that he was equally bound by canon law to allow someone else to take the burial service in his church if we wanted another clergyman to do so.'

'And do we?' enquired Amelia, beginning to wonder if perhaps after all the telephone call from England was an elaborate hoax: or even a student rag.

'We might,' responded Tod Morton frankly, 'but the late Mrs Garamond didn't.'

'Oh?' This conversation, decided Amelia, wasn't anything to do with 'Who Killed Cock Robin?' after all. It was pure *Alice in Wonderland*, that's what it was.

The undertaker was still talking. 'Mr Puckle told me that the late Mrs Garamond had asked specially in her instructions for Mr Fournier to take the funeral service.'

'Did she, indeed?' said Amelia. 'And does that mean that she knew that the rector wouldn't want to take it, then?' Like Alice she was finding that everything was getting curiouser and curiouser.

'I couldn't say, miss, I'm sure.'

'So?'

'So we've provisionally fixed the funeral for today week, miss, like I said. If it's all right with you, that is . . .'

'It's all right with me,' Amelia Kennerley heard herself saying aloud, 'but what about its being all right with everyone else?'

'Ah,' said the undertaker down the telephone line, 'the late Mrs Garamond left precise instructions about that, too.'

'Tell me . . .' commanded Amelia. There was clearly a little more to all this than met the eye.

'Very precise instructions,' said Tod Morton, proceeding to spell them out to her.

Her friend Mary-Louise had watched Amelia's face as she had listened intently, thanked the speaker, and then replaced the telephone receiver with a very thoughtful expression indeed. 'And what was all that about?' she asked Amelia.

'My great-aunt's died.'

Mary-Louise was the holiday party's language specialist and immediately said: ' "The young die sometimes, but the old always die." That's an old Breton proverb.'

Amelia restored the telephone instrument to its resting place on the *étagère*, took a deep breath, and said: 'Listen . . .'

Mary-Louise gave her her full attention.

'And,' finished Amelia presently, 'there's a notice of her death and funeral to be inserted in the principal London newspapers and two Scottish ones as well as in the three Calleshire local papers . . .'

'Naturally,' said Mary-Louise, affecting a knowledgeability she didn't really quite have yet.

'And the *Journal of the Courant Club*,' finished Amelia.

9

'The what?'

'The Courant Club.'

'Never heard of it.'

'Nor me, until this minute,' said Amelia. 'Apparently it's the house magazine for present and past employees of an outfit that she and Uncle William used to work for in the war. Some big firm or other that had something to do with manufacturing dyestuffs.' She pushed the *caquetoire* out of the sunlight and into the shaded part of the sitting room before sinking on to it. 'I say, Mary-Louise, do you know that Great-Aunt Octavia had actually drafted the death notices for the newspapers herself and left them with her solicitor all ready prepared?'

'Now that,' said Mary-Louise respectfully, 'is what I call really cool.'

'Everything there, the undertaker said, except the actual date of death.'

'Of course,' said Mary-Louise. 'I mean, you wouldn't know what date to put, would you, unless it was suicide . . .' Her voice trailed away as she was struck by an uneasy thought. 'It wasn't, Amelia, was it?'

'No,' said Amelia. 'I asked him. He said the date was blank.'

'Ah,' Mary-Louise gave a little sigh. 'I'm glad about that.'

'She also left,' went on Amelia doggedly, 'a list of those people who were to be asked back to the Grange at Great Primer after the funeral.'

'Such as . . .' That wasn't very well put, decided Mary-Louise, but she knew what she meant.

So, it seemed, did Amelia Kennerley.

'Such as the police,' said Amelia neutrally.

TWO

Oh, that a linnet should die in the spring!

'Who, sir?' asked Detective Inspector C. D. Sloan.

'You, Sloan,' barked Superintendent Leeyes.

'Me, sir?' said Sloan, who had just been summoned to his superior officer's room at 'F' Division Headquarters in Berebury.

'You heard me,' growled the superintendent.

'Yes, sir,' agreed Sloan hastily. So, probably, had half the police station. The detective inspector, known to his wife and family as Christopher Dennis and, for obvious reasons, as 'Seedy' to his friends and colleagues in the Calleshire Constabulary, was still mystified.

'Probably nothing to it, of course,' said Superintendent Leeyes largely, 'but we can't afford to take chances these days. Things aren't what they used to be.'

'No, sir.' Sloan was on safe ground in agreeing to that. He was head of the tiny Criminal Investigation Department of the Berebury Division of the county of Calleshire and all reports of such crime as there was there found their way on to his desk. 'Nothing to what, sir?'

'To this very odd invitation to a funeral that I've been trying to tell you about,' replied the superintendent unfairly. 'Some old lady's been and gone and left word with her solicitor that when she died the police were to be invited to her funeral.'

'Why?' enquired Detective Inspector Sloan.

'She didn't say why.'

11

'Sorry, sir. I meant why me in particular,' responded the detective inspector carefully. 'Do we actually know if crime is involved in any way?'

'We don't know anything, Sloan,' rejoined Leeyes testily. 'Yet, that is. We've only just heard from her solicitor. What I'm saying is that you'll have to go along to Puckle, Puckle, and Nunnery's yourself and find out if they know anything more.'

'Yes, sir.' He had, after all, had even odder assignments in his time.

'And, if they do know anything more,' he added heavily, 'whether they're prepared to tell you, which isn't the same thing by a long chalk.'

'No, sir. Very good.' Sloan reached for his notebook. 'Today week, I think you said the funeral was. In the afternoon.'

'Half past two,' the superintendent said. 'You can take Constable Crosby with you,' he went on, immediately spoiling any suspicion of magnanimity by adding, 'at least that'll get him off our backs for the afternoon.'

'Thank you, sir,' said Sloan rigidly. Detective Constable William Edward Crosby was the youngest and most jejune member of the Force in the whole of 'F' Division and usually an incubus in any police operation which did not involve driving fast cars fast.

'And there's one good thing about going to a funeral,' rumbled on Leeyes, 'that'll be a help to you both in the circumstances.'

Sloan looked up. 'Sir?'

'It isn't like a wedding where the ushers ask you whose side you're on the minute you walk in through the church door.'

'No, sir.' Crumbs of professional comfort cropped up in the strangest of places.

'Now that can be tricky,' said the superintenent, veteran of many a family reunion. 'At least at a funeral you can sit wherever you like in the church.'

It was something that Detective Inspector Sloan had not considered before.

'But if I were you, Sloan . . .'

'Sir?'

'I'd sit right at the back and keep my eyes skinned.'

'Yes, sir.' In the interests of his own Criminal Investigation Department, Sloan tried another tack with the superintendent. 'Has . . . I mean, sir, is it known if . . . er . . ., anything had occurred to the deceased that should . . . um . . . specifically call for our presence?'

'Not as far as we know to date.' The superintendent tossed a flimsy message-sheet in Sloan's direction. 'That's all the paperwork that's reached us so far.'

'Thank you, sir,' he said expressionlessly, picking it up.

'Next Friday afternoon, then, Sloan, at St Hilary's church, Great Primer . . . let me have your report in due course.'

'Yes, sir.' The detective inspector paused while he folded the paper away and then said: 'Was she by any chance ever on the Bench, this old lady?' In theory, all lay magistrates were totally detached from all policemen but it wasn't a perfect world and inevitably relationships were formed over the years of working together in the same courts. This was something that those acting for the defendants did not like at all.

'No, Sloan, she wasn't,' responded Leeyes smartly. 'I've just had that checked out myself with the magistrates' clerk.'

'It was just a thought, sir.'

'She might well have been, though,' conceded the superintendent, whose mind was following a train of reasoning that would doubtless have upset the Lord Chancellor's Department as well as nearly every defence counsel in the land. 'The Assistant Chief Constable tells me that Mrs Garamond was a bit of a nob in her own right – what the wine people call *Edelfäule*.'

'Pardon, sir?' This last must have come straight from

13

the superintendent's Wine Appreciation classes: he was a great one for attending Adult Education evening courses on all manner of subjects – the more recondite the better.

'Noble rot, Sloan. Noble rot.'

'Ah.'

What the assistant chief constable – that most well connected of men – had actually said was that the late Mrs Octavia Garamond was one of the few surviving members of the old school, coming as she did from the ancient Scottish family of Harquil-Grasset. That was before he had quoted something melancholy of G. K. Chesterton's about the last sad squires who ride slowly down to the sea; but Superintendent Leeyes had grasped the essentials.

'He said something else, too, Sloan.'

'Sir?'

'That it was an interesting old church out there at Great Primer . . .'

'Really, sir?' said Sloan politely.

'From a police procedural point of view, that is.'

'How come, sir?'

'You may well ask,' grumbled Leeyes, who didn't hold with having toffee-nosed assistant chief constables in the Force anyway.

'Stolen chalices?' advanced Sloan. The aristocratic assistant chief constable wouldn't have found wayward clergymen interesting, that was for sure.

'Something historical,' sniffed Leeyes, spiritual brother of the late Henry Ford.

'Sir?' Perhaps, then, thought Sloan, in days gone by the luckless incumbent out there at Great Primer had been sent to gaol for offences against the Public Worship Regulation Act of 1874: heinous activities like lighting candles where lighted candles there should not be. Their lecturer at the Police Training College had insisted to a

14

disbelieving class of young policeman that ritualism had always been good for a real parochial dust-up . . .

'Some marks on the south wall,' said Superintendent Leeyes sourly. The assistant chief constable might have been an antiquarian: the superintendent was not.

'Really, sir?'

'Reputed,' snorted Leeyes, 'to be a thirteenth-century mark designating the boundary of the ancient parish Watch and Ward of Great Primer for the village constable.'

'I'll look out for it, sir,' promised Detective Inspector Sloan solemnly, adding in the same tone, 'Do we happen, by any chance, to know the cause of Mrs Garamond's death?'

'Ha!' exclaimed Leeyes. 'We know what her doctor put on the death certificate, Sloan, which may or may not be the same thing at all.'

'Point taken, sir.' To say that the superintendent accorded the senior of the healing professions any reverence would have been an over-statement: he was a medical heretic of deep conviction and long standing. 'What did the doctor put, then?'

'Left ventricular failure,' said the superintendent. 'It's there on that paper I gave you just now.'

'Usually a natural cause,' observed Detective Inspector Sloan drily.

'And senile myocardial degeneration.'

'So she was old . . .' murmured Sloan, half-aloud.

'Age is relative,' declared Leeyes, a man within sight of his own retirement. He paused and then said: 'There is, though, just one odd thing about the death certificate – or, rather, about the circumstances in which the registered general medical practitioner signed it . . .'

'Sir?' Detective Inspector Sloan was immediately all ears, his attention wholly engaged now.

'The deceased had particularly asked her doctor to

make a complete examination of her body after she had died. Made quite a point of it, Dr Aldus said.'

'In fact, gentlemen,' Dr John Aldus repeated to Detective Inspector Sloan and Detective Constable Crosby, when they were both sitting in his consulting rooms later that afternoon, 'in this matter I may tell you Mrs Octavia Garamond had been specific to the point of bluntness.'

There were noises off in the background; somewhere a baby was crying and nearer at hand a telephone ringing. Nevertheless Detective Inspector Sloan leaned forward and invited the general practitioner to tell him exactly how it had been.

'What she said to me on one of my last visits to her,' recounted John Aldus, 'was: "You'll examine me properly, doctor, won't you, when I've died?" '

'I'll make quite sure you're dead,' John Aldus had promised, wondering if Mrs Garamond was going to ask him to open one of her veins to make death absolutely sure. A lot of his elderly patients had a morbid – and quite unjustified – fear of being buried alive.

'That's not what I meant at all,' the old lady had said severely. 'Dammit, man, if you can't recognize death by this time then you've no business to be on your sort of income.'

He had said: 'Then what do you mean?' taking her frankness in good part. Like most medical practitioners he spent a lot of his time trying to interpret the oblique remarks made to him by his patients and like all medical practitioners he had learnt to deal – and deal well – in euphemism. Old Mrs Garamond's bluntness made a refreshing change.

'What I mean,' she had said straightly, 'is that I want you to examine my corpse. Is that clear enough for you?'

Dr Aldus had been torn between being professionally soothing and naturally intrigued. 'Of course I will,' he said gently, 'if you want me to.'

16

'I do. And properly, mind you. None of this just pulling back the sheet for a quick look.'

'Tell me why . . .'

The old lady had given a high cackle and said: 'Queen Victoria's doctor thought he knew his patient.'

'Ah.'

'It wasn't until she died that he discovered that she had had a ventral hernia.'

'You haven't got a ventral hernia.'

Mrs Octavia Garamond had given him an enigmatic smile which had stuck in his mind ever since. 'I know that.'

'Then why,' he had asked, 'are you so anxious that I examine you after death?'

She had refused to be drawn. 'Put it down, doctor, if you like,' she said wheezily, 'to honouring an old woman's last request.'

'Very well.' John Aldus would have humoured her anyway, but, genuinely concerned now, he had asked: 'Is there anything worrying you, m'dear?'

Her answer had been totally unexpected.

'Hell, doctor, hell . . .' She coughed.

It had been a peffing cough, a heart cough, not a chesty one.

'There may be no such place—' he had begun: but by then Octavia Garamond had not been really listening to him.

'You remember what Ariel said, doctor, in *The Tempest* . . .'

'Tell me.'

' "Hell is empty, and all the devils are here . . .",' she had quoted rather breathlessly.

' "Hell is empty",' he repeated after her.

'Shakespeare knew.'

'Oh, yes.' The doctor was with her there. 'William Shakespeare knew all right, especially after his son, Hamnet, died.'

' "Hell is empty, and all the devils are here",' she said again, closing her eyes and losing interest in the rest of the consultation.

THREE

Bury him, comrades, in pitiful duty.

Now, somewhere in the background of the doctor's surgery, the telephone began to ring again. The baby had stopped crying, but there were other noises off. Dr Aldus looked intently across at the two policemen sitting in his consulting room and continued his narrative.

'I arranged for Mrs Garamond to have an oxygen cylinder by her bedside to help her breathlessness but that was all I could get out of her, gentlemen, except . . .'

'Yes?' said Sloan attentively.

' . . . Except that she did say to me on my next visit to her that she thought that her soul was going to be required of her one night quite soon.'

Sloan looked up.

The doctor went on: 'I remember she quoted some fearsome old ballad to me about coming to Purgatory's fire at last.' He frowned. 'I think she said it was from "The Lyke-Wake Dirge".' He shook his head. 'There was no comforting her.'

'And was it?' Detective Constable Crosby leant forward with what seemed like genuine interest. 'Her soul required of her soon, I mean?'

'Within the week,' replied the doctor tersely.

Detective Inspector Sloan cleared his throat and asked if the doctor had prescribed anything specifically for his patient's fear of hell-fire.

'I'm afraid there's no nostrum in the *British Pharmaco-*

poeia which'll treat that, Inspector. At least,' he added drily, 'not quite so late in the day as this.'

'Quite so,' said Sloan smoothly. There had been a couplet that had stuck in his mind since his schooldays which offered quite the opposite view:

Twixt the stirrup and the ground
Mercy I ask'd, and mercy found.

But he forbore to quote it. The sentiment was for incurable romantics, not for unimaginative general practitioners; or even, come to that, for hard-bitten detective inspectors.

The baby started to cry again.

'Only a quietus,' Dr Aldus was still continuing his own line of thought, 'and I can assure you that I didn't give her one of those.'

'Quite . . .' murmured Sloan, making a note to check, all the same.

'I'm only a country doctor,' rumbled on John Aldus, 'not a priest.'

'Confession is good for the soul,' remarked Crosby chattily.

Aldus turned to the constable and said: 'So it may be, but doctors don't deal in absolution – not if they've got any sense, that is.' He frowned. 'Besides . . .'

'Yes?' prompted Sloan.

'Mrs Garamond was on quite enough medication as it was anyway. Quite enough.'

'For her heart?' said Sloan: it wasn't for her fear of hell, then.

'For her heart,' said the doctor flatly. 'There's no treatment for growing old yet, Inspector, although people have been looking for the elixir of youth long enough.'

'True,' agreed Sloan, who was only nearly old enough to be interested in the subject.

'Ageing is a process, not a disease,' Aldus went on, 'although I dare say a treatment for even that will come along one of these fine days.' He grimaced. 'But not in my time, I hope.'

Detective Inspector Sloan had another, quite different, question for the medical man. 'This last request of the deceased, doctor, did you carry it out?'

'As a matter of fact, Inspector, I did – even though it isn't usual when there isn't going to be a cremation.'

'Why?'

Aldus hesitated. 'Because she asked me to, I suppose; because I was curious perhaps; because . . .'

'Because she was there?' suggested Detective Constable Crosby unexpectedly. 'Like Everest?'

'That, too, I suppose.' If Aldus was surprised by the simile, he did not let it show. 'But, like us all, principally in case I'd missed something.'

'And had you?' enquired the detective constable insouciantly, while Sloan listened carefully. The fear of having missed something important was one thing which all true detectives shared with the medical profession: and the agony of finding this out too late was common to both callings.

'Not that I could see,' said John Aldus. 'All that I found when I examined her was the body of an anile woman, wasted as I would have expected in one so old, a little oedematous still in spite of diuretics – you don't see anasarca much these days – and very slightly cyanosed.'

Sloan leant forward. 'Tell me, doctor, what might there have been?'

The general practitioner looked slightly abashed. 'I must confess, Inspector, that it did just cross my mind – I know it sounds silly – that I might just find something that Mrs Garamond hadn't wanted me to know about in life.'

'Like Queen Victoria?' asked Crosby intelligently.

Aldus nodded slowly. 'In a way.'

'Like what exactly?' persisted Sloan.

'It had occurred to me,' said the doctor somewhat defensively, 'that I might just conceivably find something ineradicable on her skin . . .'

'Like a tattoo?' said Sloan.

The baby which had been crying in the background suddenly stopped. Into the silence the doctor said quietly: 'Like a concentration-camp number.'

Sloan jerked his head. 'The Mark of Cain.'

'It wasn't too far-fetched a thought, Inspector,' said Aldus. 'I remember being told by someone – not by Mrs Garamond, though – that she'd done something unusual by way of war-work, although I never knew quite what.'

'Ah,' said Sloan, who knew that even now there were still closed books in some offices of state.

'She'd been married to a very distinguished scientist, too, and she'd been an educated woman herself,' said Aldus. 'I did know that – besides you only had to talk to her . . . For all I knew, Inspector, she might have been caught abroad when the war began. Or gone there after it had started.'

'But you didn't find anything like that, did you, doctor?' persisted Sloan.

'No,' he said, shaking his head. 'Just, like Christian, old scars to bear with her into the next world. Big enough ones, mind you. Appendix and gall-bladder, I should have said at a guess. Surgeons weren't so tidy with their incisions in the old days. No key-hole surgery then.'

'Any bruises?' asked Detective Inspector Sloan prosaically, even though he, too, knew his *Pilgrim's Progress*.

'No.' Dr John Aldus hunched his shoulders forward. 'And I didn't find anything in her mouth either when I examined that.'

Detective Constable Crosby came to life. 'Her mouth?'

'If you ask me,' said the doctor with apparent irrel-

22

evance, 'there are plenty more old ladies killed by suffo-
cation by their exhausted carers than you people or their
doctors ever know about.'

Detective Inspector Sloan did not dispute that. He had
always suspected that 'losing a pillow-fight' had another
meaning in many an unsatisfactory nursing home for the
elderly.

The doctor was still recounting his actions. 'I checked
her tablets, too, just to be on the safe side. I wouldn't
have put it past her to take the lot if she'd had a mind
to . . .'

So, noted Sloan promptly, Dr John Aldus, registered
medical practitioner, in spite of what he had just said,
had been sufficiently impressed by his patient's last request to make assurance doubly sure in some respects
at least.

'They were beside her bed but they were all present
and correct,' said Aldus. 'Moreover, she hadn't vomited
at all.'

'Who had been looking after her?' asked Sloan.

'A series of women from an agency in Calleford did
the care side and my practice nurse looked in on her
every other day. She gave her a blanket bath and so forth,
and she had never noticed anything untoward . . .'

Sloan made a mental note, though, that the good
doctor had already seen fit to ask her.

'That's only since Mrs Garamond's old maid died, of
course.' Aldus looked at Sloan. 'Until then she had
always had Ellen. I may say that Ellen was the archetypal
ancient retainer and she used to do everything for her.'

Crosby suddenly came to life again and asked very
promptly: 'And what did Ellen die from, then?' Like the
archetypal family retainer that she had evidently been,
Ellen did not appear to have had a surname.

'I can't tell you that.' Aldus waved a hand in a roughly
eastward direction. 'She died over in Luston while she

was visiting her niece. That's where she came from, Luston.'

'That must have been a bit of a blow for your patient,' observed Sloan.

The general practitioner hesitated. 'I treat a great many old people, Inspector, and my experience is that the older people are the better they take that sort of thing.'

'I can see that they might.'

'And when they are very old, then they just have to think only of themselves – it's a sort of protective selfishness. We're talking about the survivors, of course.' He paused and then added thoughtfully, 'I don't know if there's a moral in that . . .'

'Probably,' said Sloan, who had been taught at an early age by a church-going mother all about there being sermons in stones.

'That is not to say, naturally, that Mrs Garamond didn't grieve about Ellen. She'd been with her for years and I'm sure she'd have been treated uncommonly well.'

'What about family?' said Sloan, policeman first, last, and all the time when working. In his experience where there was a death there was usually a relative.

'Certainly none that I knew of,' responded the doctor promptly, 'and Ellen did tell me on one occasion that Mrs Garamond had been alone in the world for quite a long time.'

'Outlived them all, had she?' said Sloan, not unsympathetically. These were the owners of houses which eventually the police had to break into, where no one ever called, where the telephone never rang and no post came . . . where only the milkman provided a link with the outside world.

'Must have done,' agreed the doctor. 'My patient once told me that she knew more people in the churchyard than in the village these days.'

'And,' said Detective Inspector Sloan, getting back to

24

the nub of the matter, 'you expected her to die when she did?'

'I wouldn't have been surprised if she'd died at any time,' replied Aldus frankly, 'but you never can tell with heart cases, quite apart from the capacity of some old ladies to go on living almost for ever.'

'So, then, doctor,' Sloan glanced down at his notebook, 'you were quite happy to issue a death certificate in this case?'

'I was then.' Unexpectedly he added, 'I'm not now.'

The telephone had started to ring again somewhere not far from the consulting room. It sounded like a tocsin.

'Why?' Sloan raised an eyebrow.

'For two reasons, Inspector.'

Sloan leant forward. 'Yes?'

Dr Aldus drummed his fingers on the desk in front of him. 'I don't know which to put first.'

'Either will do,' said the policeman evenly.

'One reason is because you are here.'

'And the other?' prompted Sloan.

'The second reason,' said the doctor steadily, 'is that I had cause to believe that I might have had a pecuniary interest in my patient's death . . .'

'Had you, indeed?' murmured Sloan.

'And her solicitor . . . that's James Puckle – young James, that is – hasn't denied it. I asked him when I heard that the police were coming to see me and he wouldn't say I hadn't.'

FOUR

Muffle the dinner bell, solemnly ring.

'Now just let me get this quite straight, Sloan,' said Dr Dabbe.

Since it was way past six o'clock in the evening and a Friday evening to boot, the two policemen had made their way out into the country to the home of the Consultant Pathologist to the Berebury and District Hospital Management Trust. They were sitting in the pathologist's study while Detective Inspector Sloan explained the case of the late Mrs Octavia Garamond to him.

'Am I to understand, then,' carried on the pathologist, 'that the police want me to perform a post-mortem examination solely on the strength of an old lady having expressed a wish to her general practitioner that he carries out a superficial – and I use the word in its exact sense – examination of her body after death?'

'There is also,' said Sloan sturdily, 'the deceased's written request, lodged with her solicitors, that the police be invited to the funeral.' It was not often that he got the chance to beard the pathologist in his own den but Dr Dabbe had left his laboratory and gone home for the weekend. 'Mrs Garamond died, we think, in the early hours of this morning . . .'

'Funnily enough,' continued the pathologist sedulously, 'John Aldus, the general practitioner concerned, now wants me to do the same thing . . .'

'Does he indeed?' said Sloan alertly.

'Because he says that he's now fairly sure that he stands to get a legacy under the last Will and Testament of the aforementioned old lady.'

'I'm seeing her solicitor first thing tomorrow morning,' said Sloan, casting an interested eye through the study window and out into the garden beyond. The roses, he noted, at Pennyless Bench needed dead-heading rather badly. Crosby's attention, though, had been attracted to a row of specimen jars on the mantelpiece. Where other men might have had ornaments or college trophies – or even a clock – there were standing a series of clear glass vessels in which were suspended what looked like spectacularly unhappy pickled gherkins.

'There's no law, Sloan, that I know of against a doctor being a legatee,' said Dr Dabbe, who was also a doctor but, if his untended roses were anything to go by, Sloan decided, definitely not a gardener.

'None,' said Detective Inspector Sloan blandly.

'Moreover, I gather that you've already talked old Locombe-Stapleford into agreeing with you . . .'

'The Coroner,' quoted Sloan demurely, 'felt that a post-mortem examination was indicated in the best interests of everyone concerned.'

'If you really mean everyone,' the pathologist gave a wolfish grin and said pedantically, 'then I would have thought myself that that rather depended on what I found, wouldn't you?'

'True, doctor,' said Sloan, 'very true.'

'And,' said the pathologist, this time with a dead-pan expression, 'you've come over here after hours on a Friday evening to tell me this, or was it just a pleasant evening for a run?'

'I just happened,' said Sloan guilelessly, 'to hear the weather forecast for the weekend.'

'Perfect for sailing,' growled the pathologist who kept

his Westerly Longbow at the marina at Kinnisport. 'Even the tides are right.'

'That's what we thought, too, doctor.'

'You might even say, Sloan' – here Dr Dabbe gave the barometer a rueful tap – 'in the immortal words of the bard, "Fair stood the wind for France".'

Sloan coughed. 'It's actually, doctor, in a manner of speaking the wind . . . er . . . from France that we're more interested in at the moment.'

The pathologist looked up. Detective Constable Crosby appeared to be engaged in counting the specimen jars on the pathologist's mantelpiece.

'We contacted the Coroner,' said Sloan, 'because Mrs Garamond's sole executrix, who is the only living relative of the deceased known to her solicitors, Puckle, Puckle, and Nunnery . . .'

'No shortage of relatives in that firm, is there?' observed Detective Constable Crosby to no one in particular.

'Is,' persevered Sloan, 'a young woman called Amelia Kennerley.'

'And she's hardly a relative, is she?' said Crosby. 'Doctor, what's in those jars you've got over there?'

'Paralytic ileuses,' said the pathologist. 'I collect them, you know. Marvellous specimens, aren't they?'

'Amelia Kennerley,' said Sloan concisely, refusing to be deflected, 'is a great-niece of the deceased's late husband.'

'Collect them?' echoed Crosby.

'When I come across them, of course,' said Dr Dabbe modestly. 'Little hobby of mine.'

'She is *en route* to Calleshire at this moment from the Dordogne,' said Sloan, 'and so couldn't be contacted and invited to give her consent to the post-mortem being carried out.'

'Are all of the people those bits belonged to dead?'

asked Crosby, still fascinated by the contents of the jars on the mantelpiece.

'Oh, yes. Very,' replied the pathologist cheerfully. 'Now then, Sloan, tell me, are we using this autopsy as the final arbiter of clinical practice or do you really think there's more to it than that?'

'I don't know, doctor. We haven't got any more to go on than I've already told you.' He stood up, ready to take his leave. 'I understand that the deceased had known for some time that she wasn't getting any better and had told her solicitor so.'

'Ah, that was probably only to get him to get a move on with writing her Will for her,' said Dr Dabbe, but he said it without conviction.

'My late client's exact words, as I remember, Inspector,' said James Puckle, 'were "like to die".'

The offices, down by the bridge, of Puckle, Puckle, and Nunnery, Notaries Public, had been built in the early part of the eighteenth century. As the partner who specialized in matters to do with the Town and Country Planning Acts (and a man old before his time if ever there was one), was fond of pointing out, there were tell-tale signs on the façade of their building by which the experts knew this.

There was, for instance, a string course at roof-level which had become law in 1707 by virtue of the Second London Fire Act calling for the replacement of the old wooden cornices and modillions that had so accelerated the spread of the Great Fire of London in 1666.

' "Like to die"?' Detective Inspector Sloan duly entered the words into his notebook.

The building fashion first set in London had taken its time to reach the sleepy little market town of Berebury, deep in rural Calleshire, but it had got there in the end. It had soon been followed by visible evidence of the implementation of the new law requiring the universal recessing of window frames by the statutory three inches, another measure planned to delay the advance of fire in timber and brick buildings.

Detective Inspector Sloan was not interested in windows. To him the building just looked old.

James Puckle, though, still had his mind harking further back in history than the Great Fire of London.

' "Like to die", Inspector,' he said, 'is just one of the expressions that used to be very common in the preamble to a great many medieval Wills.'

'Really, sir?' There was only one last Will and Testament in which Sloan was interested just at this moment and that belonged to Octavia Garamond.

'Another very popular one was "written nigh unto death".' The solicitor – he wasn't very old himself and looked rather out of place in these archaic surroundings – glanced across at the two policemen and said: 'You see, Inspector, in times gone by our ancestors usually knew when they were going to die . . .'

'Or had been told,' put in Sloan.

'Or had been told,' concurred Puckle, 'and they weren't mealy-mouthed about it as we are in our day and age.'

'Called a grave-digger's spade a sexton's shovel, did they?' said Detective Constable Crosby, who was finding his chair uncomfortable.

'I don't mean, though, Inspector,' said James Puckle, diplomatically sticking to the point, 'to give the impression that Mrs Garamond's was a death-bed Will, because it wasn't.' He steepled his fingers and assumed a solemn expression, immediately looking much older. 'Death-bed Wills,' he pronounced solemnly, 'are usually bad Wills.'

'I can see that they might be,' agreed Sloan, remembering that the great Dr Samuel Johnson had said that when a man knows he is to be hanged in a fortnight, it concentrates his mind wonderfully. A death-bed sounded a much quicker proposition to him.

'The profession doesn't like them at all,' went on James Puckle. 'Working against the clock doesn't make for considered thought.'

'More haste, less speed,' said Detective Constable Crosby helpfully.

Detective Inspector Sloan, who worked against the clock all the time, did not say anything at all.

'Quite apart from that,' said the solicitor, 'I can assure you that my client had given a great deal – I think I may say, a very great deal – of consideration to her – er – testamentary dispositions.'

'I'm glad to hear it,' said Sloan, the writing of Wills being, in his view, like the marriage contract, and not something to be entered into lightly and unadvisedly.

'In fact, I think you might like to know, gentlemen,' said James Puckle, 'that Mrs Garamond's last Will and Testament was dated almost two years ago.'

Sloan tried to look suitably grateful for this less than riveting disclosure.

'When it was drawn up by my grandfather,' said James Puckle.

Sloan said: 'I remember him well . . .' It wasn't like living in a big city; in small country towns policemen really got to know solicitors.

'And he was the executor of it as well,' said Puckle.

'Let me see, sir, he must have died a year or more ago now . . .'

'Nearly two,' said James Puckle.

'So . . ?'

'So Mrs Garamond executed a codicil . . .'

'Appointing Amelia Kennerley instead?' said Sloan.

'And revoking the charging clause as well,' nodded Puckle regretfully.

Sloan looked up, asking bluntly, 'Why?' There was,

after all, no shortage of Puckles in the firm, to say nothing of Charles Nunnery, who was, to Sloan's certain knowledge of the Magistrates' Court, still going strong.

'Mrs Garamond – er – took against the remaining partners for some reason and appointed Miss Kennerley in my grandfather's place . . .'

Sloan's note this time was a mental one. It would be committed to his notebook later.

'My father – he was senior partner by then – advised Mrs Garamond most strongly of the unwisdom of entrusting the winding-up of an estate like hers to one so young. Moreover,' he added significantly, 'to someone quite unknown to her.'

'And,' pointed out Sloan, making a note now, 'someone who wasn't strictly speaking even a relative.'

'Precisely, Inspector. But I understand from my father that our client was adamant in this matter.' He suddenly looked quite boyish and grinned as he said: 'Actually I found Mrs Garamond rather more than quite adamant in all matters.'

'If,' remarked Detective Constable Crosby out of the blue, 'she was "Like to die" two years ago, then she took her time about it, didn't she?'

'The last time I saw Mrs Garamond,' said the solicitor, 'she quoted King Charles II to me.'

'The Merry Monarch,' said Sloan, dredging something up from a classroom memory.

' "A merry monarch, scandalous and poor" was what they said about him,' rejoined James Puckle instantly, 'but what my client said to me then was that she was, like Charles II, "being an unconscionable time a–dying".'

'She wasn't like him, poor, though, was she?' ventured Detective Inspector Sloan, policeman rather than historian any day.

'Oh, dear me, no, Inspector. On the contrary, in fact . . .' He paused. 'Quite on the contrary, I should say.'

'Money talks,' observed Detective Constable Crosby to nobody in particular.

Sloan leaned forward slightly and said to the solicitor: 'Do you have any information at all, Mr Puckle, as to why the police should have been invited to attend Octavia Garamond's funeral?'

He shook his head. 'None. It was merely one of a number of actions enjoined upon us by our client . . .'

Once a client, always a client, thought Sloan, was obviously a watchword at the firm of Puckle, Puckle, and Nunnery. Even if the charging clause had been revoked.

'Scheduled to take effect as soon as she died, including the placing of her obituary notices in various specified newspapers. This, you understand, Inspector, was in case Miss Kennerley could not be located before the funeral or declined to act as sole executrix.'

'You mean,' said Crosby with something like animation, 'that she hadn't said she would?'

'I mean,' said James Puckle, 'that she hadn't been asked.'

'That's funny for a start,' said the constable.

The mind of Detective Inspector Sloan though was working along quite different lines. 'These requests that Mrs Garamond left with you, Mr Puckle . . .'

'Yes?'

'Were there any other instructions that we don't know about?' He paused and added, 'And should?'

James Puckle said carefully: 'One, perhaps.'

Detective Inspector Sloan said nothing at all rather loudly.

Almost as if he were talking to himself the solicitor murmured, 'I see no harm in mentioning – perhaps I should anyway – that there was an instruction that the executrix . . .'

'Amelia Kennerley.'

'Was to be given the key to the Grange at Great Primer before anyone else at all went in there . . .'

FIVE

Bury him kindly, up in the corner;

The key, neatly labelled, was the first thing that Amelia Kennerley set eyes on when she entered her own home after arriving back from France on the Saturday morning. It was lying on the hall table, with a letter addressed to her beside it. From beyond, further through the house, she could hear a coffee percolator thumping away and, if the sound of piano music was anything to go by, a lady doctor at play.

'If you want a bath first, I'll turn the coffee off,' called out the musician.

'Coffee, coffee, my kingdom for a cup of coffee.' Amelia went straight through the hall to the kitchen. 'I never did think that Richard III had his priorities right.'

A tousled iron-grey head appeared round the kitchen door. 'There's grapefruit in the larder if you want it.'

'What I want,' said Amelia firmly, 'is to be told what's going on.'

'Can't help you much there, I'm afraid.' Phoebe Plantin ran her broad, capable fingers through her untidy hair, rumpling it still further. 'And your father's in South America. Not that he would be able to help all that much either. He never mentioned the Garamonds to me that I remember.'

'Or me,' said Amelia regretfully. 'Where in South America? Did he say?'

'Somewhere in the Matto Grosso,' replied Dr Plantin, 'with a tribe called the Pegola.'

34

'Up-country?'

'You know your father. With him it's always up-country.'

'True.' Amelia used to describe her father as absent-minded until Phoebe Plantin had explained that he wasn't absentminded at all, but single-minded, which was quite different but had the same effect.

'Not only, you will be pleased to hear,' said Dr Plantin, 'do the Pegola South American Indians have a very unusual and interesting class structure untouched by the outside world but they are also said to have what is thought to be a unique method of communicating with each other without speech round the mountains.'

'Irresistible,' agreed Amelia.

'I don't think he actually tried to resist it,' said Professor Kennerley's second wife without rancour. 'He went as soon as he could.'

Amelia grinned. She had only been ten years old when her own mother had died and it had been ages afterwards before the significance of something that she had heard her mother, Helena, say when she was very ill had dawned on Amelia. Helena Kennerley, who had been a great friend of Phoebe Plantin's as well as her patient, had known full well that she was going to die.

One day Amelia had overheard her mother say to Phoebe: 'You'll look after both my pretty chickens, won't you, love?'

Even now Amelia had not forgotten Phoebe's speechless, deeply moved, nod, but it had been much, much later before she realized that her mother had been quoting the bereaved Macduff in Shakespeare's *Macbeth*, and even later still before it dawned on her that Helena Kennerley had been meaning to say that in some ways her husband was more child than man.

'One of Puckles' clerks came round earlier with the key of the Grange for you,' Phoebe informed her, 'and an appointment with the firm first thing Monday morning as they thought you'd need it.'

Amelia scanned the letter from the solicitors and then said: 'Phoebe, is this your weekend off duty by any chance?'

'It is, praise be. Not another spotty child or running nose until Monday morning.'

'Then please could you take me over to Great Primer later on? When I've had a chance to have a bath and grabbed something to eat?'

'Surely.' One of Dr Phoebe Plantin's great virtues as a stepmother was that she not only never made helpful suggestions but always fell in with those of other people when she could. 'The Grange shouldn't be too difficult to find. Oh, and by the way, Tod Morton, the undertaker, called as well. He wants you to give him a ring when you can, even though it's out of hours . . .'

Another place which did not keep office hours was the mortuary.

It was the middle of one of the sunniest Saturday afternoons of the year when Dr Dabbe welcomed Detective Inspector Sloan and Detective Constable Crosby to the post-mortem laboratory. Burns, Dr Dabbe's perennially silent post-mortem room technician, jerked his head in their direction by way of greeting.

'Come along into the Temple of Truth, gentlemen,' said the pathologist, 'where all shall be revealed and I'll tell you which of the three causes of death it was that actually killed . . . Octavia Garamond, did you say her name was?'

'Three?' queried Detective Inspector Sloan rather sharply. In his book there had always been four causes of death: natural causes, accident, suicide, and homicide. 'Only three, Doctor?'

'Only three, Sloan.' The doctor held up a bony finger.

'Firstly, disease . . . what William Shakespeare described in his splendid statement on genetics as "the thousand ills the flesh is heir to". Burns, my gown . . .'

'Naturally. I can see that.'

'Secondly, there's medical treatment.'

'Medical treatment?' echoed Detective Constable Crosby naïvely.

'Otherwise known as iatrogenic disease,' said the pathologist. 'Or diseases caused by doctors. There's a lot of it about.' He turned round while Burns tied his gown.

'Comes from keeping on taking the tablets, I suppose,' said Sloan drily, 'prescribed for the aforementioned diseases.'

'Or even,' went on the pathologist with deep cynicism, 'for the wrong disease. Burns, my gloves.'

'And thirdly?' asked Sloan. He thought that the medical profession had a famous precept about first doing no harm but he didn't like to say so at this point.

'Thirdly's diagnosis,' finished Dr Dabbe laconically. He held out his hands for the rubber surgical gloves.

Detective Constable Crosby, prepared to postpone the post-mortem for as long as he could, said: 'How can you die of a diagnosis then, doctor?'

'Happens all the time,' said Dabbe, waving one gloved hand. The other hand he held out in front of him. 'Now, this one, Burns.'

'How come?' said Crosby.

Colloquial English, decided Detective Inspector Sloan, was all very well for the police station canteen but he was in two minds about apologizing to the doctor for Crosby's use of it here and to him when Dr Dabbe responded directly to the constable.

'First, Crosby, your doctor tells you that you've got the dreaded lurgies.'

'So?' responded Crosby.

'So,' said the pathologist, in no whit put out, 'you get

hold of an out-of-date medical dictionary and read up all about the lurgies.'

'And?' said Crosby, even more informally.

Detective Inspector Sloan winced: young constables got brasher and brasher.

'And you learn from the old dictionary,' carried on Dr Dabbe, 'that patients who have the dreaded lurgies don't get better.'

'Like the people whose innards are in those glass things you've got?' said Crosby.

'Exactly,' concluded the pathologist cheerfully, 'so you go home and turn up your toes, too.'

Crosby knitted his brows. 'Sort of witch-doctors but the other way round?'

'I think,' said Detective Inspector Sloan austerely, 'we can take it that Mrs Garamond did not die of her diagnosis. We're ready when you are, doctor.'

Gowned and gloved, the pathologist advanced purposefully towards the body of an anonymous-looking old woman, a handwritten ticket tied to her right big toe the only visible sign of her having had an identity at all. 'If I could have a motto over the door here it would be *Mortui Vivos Docenti*,' Dabbe said.

'We're got a blue lamp over ours,' remarked Crosby, who did not enjoy attending post-mortems.

Sloan, who said nothing, found his mind had wandered from the mortuary to a certain spot in Calleford Minster. The body of old Octavia Garamond reminded him of nothing so much as one of those ancient tombs in the Minster where a long-dead prelate was shown in effigy on a table tomb at eye level in all his mitred glory, while lying underneath he was depicted as bare cadaver, the moral drawn in alabaster for all to see. There was no mitred glory about the late Mrs Garamond now.

Dr Dabbe stood immobile beside the post-mortem table and said: 'You should treat the dead patient just like the living, Sloan. Did you know that?'

'No, doctor.'

'Use your eyes first, your hands next, and your tongue last. If at all.'

'Yes, doctor.'

Dabbe peered over the deceased's face – and broke his own rule. 'Something a bit odd here, Sloan . . .'

'Where, doctor?'

'Round her nose and mouth. Look for yourself.' The pathologist pointed to a thin ring of pressure marks which were only just visible.

'She'd been having oxygen,' said Sloan.

'Which might account for it,' agreed Dabbe, continuing with his visual examination. 'No other signs of abnormality on head or neck. Make a note of that, will you, Burns?' The pathologist took a step or two to the right. 'And nothing on the chest. There are two scars on the abdomen – signs of old surgical assaults . . .'

It was interesting, thought Sloan, to learn that the medical profession as well as the patient considered surgery as an assault.

'Cholecystectomy, I should say – do you know, Sloan, that they do it with mirrors these days – I know, tell me it reflects them great credit – and down here, at a guess, a very old appendectomy . . . more of a laparotomy, really. The surgeon can't have known what he was looking for when he went in there. The really fancy surgeons don't take the appendix out nowadays – comes in handy for spare parts later, you see . . .'

'Really, doctor?' The detective inspector leaned forward politely and took a look. John Bunyan had been right when he had caused Mr Standfast to say at the end of *Pilgrim's Progress*: 'My scars I take with me to the other side.' Perhaps – who could say? – that was all anyone ever took with them into Kingdom Come . . .

'Big enough for him to have got both his hands in up to the elbows, I would have thought,' said Dr Dabbe straightening up. 'Tell me, is there anything you think I should be particularly looking out for in the case of' – the pathologist squinted down at the parcel label attached to an elderly *digitus maximus* and read aloud – 'Octavia Louise Augustina Garamond?'

'The death certificate says . . .' began Sloan and left the sentence unfinished. The pathologist's expression showed exactly what he thought about death certificates.

'I've seen it,' Dabbe said, giving his rubber gloves an extra onward tug and reaching for a scalpel. 'Do you know that three quarters of all necroscopies disclose previously unknown and clinically important findings? Now, then . . .'

It was a full hour before he pulled his gloves off again.

When he spoke it was to Burns, his technician. 'What have you got down so far?'

'Oedema of the brain and lungs, doctor, dilation of the heart with fatty degeneration of the myocardium . . .'

'Aldus got that bit right anyway,' said Dabbe. 'Go on . . .'

'Yes, doctor.' Burns read out: 'Fatty infiltration of the liver and congestion of the spleen and kidneys. Samples of all organs taken.'

The pathologist nodded and started to take his gown off. 'I'll be showing this case at our next Mortality Meeting, Sloan, as one of great clinical interest.'

'Oh, yes, doctor?' said Sloan, adding, with a caution born over the years, 'And in what way is it interesting?'

'The cause of death . . .'

'Yes, doctor?' Sloan had his pen ready now. 'What was it?'

For the very first time ever, in his memory, Dr Dabbe said to Sloan: 'Not ascertained.'

' "Not ascertained"?' echoed Sloan. Even the phlegmatic Burns paused in his duties and looked up. Crosby was still looking at his shoes.

'Perhaps when the reports on some of the sections I've

taken come back,' said the pathologist, tossing his gown into the bin, 'I may be in a position to tell you more. In the mean time . . .'

'Yes?' said Sloan.

'I fear I can't help you any further, and I shall tell the Coroner so.'

'Not ascertained?' echoed the superintendent indignantly down the telephone line. He, at least, had gone home for the weekend. 'What does he mean, Sloan? That he doesn't know?'

'That he can't find out,' said Sloan.

'I thought they were using post-mortems for quality control these days,' said Leeyes unhelpfully.

'He's put on his report,' said Sloan reading carefully, 'that he's now going to await the outcome of some diagnostic paraffin-section histopathology.'

'Nice work, if you can get it, I suppose,' grumbled Leeyes. 'All the pathologist can tell us, then, is that it isn't all that obvious what knocked the old party off?'

'He doesn't usually say he doesn't know,' pointed out Sloan.

'Makes a nice change, does that,' said Leeyes. 'And what are you going to do now? Got an appointment with a rose, have you, Sloan?'

'No, sir. I was hoping for a quiet weekend, though . . .'

In which hope he could not have been more disappointed.

'Just wanted a quick word, miss,' said Tod Morton over the telephone. 'I thought I might catch you before you went out to Great Primer. I wanted to let you know that I've had the rector on the blo— line.'

Amelia frowned. 'A Mr Fournier, wasn't it?'

41

'That's right, miss. Seems as if he went round to the Grange yesterday afternoon to leave you a note asking whether you would want an organist and the church choir and so forth at the funeral . . .'

'Probably,' said Amelia.

'And he met a young woman walking away from the Grange as he arrived. She had some flowers and said she'd come to try to see Mrs Garamond.'

Amelia murmured under her breath, ' "Too Late the Phalarope", I'm afraid.'

'I didn't quite catch that, miss,' said Tod. 'Anyway, the rector told her to get in touch with me seeing as he didn't know anything about you, does he?'

'No . . .' said Amelia, catching his drift.

'Anyway, this woman asked when the funeral was going to be, and I told her. Very upset she was, too, miss. She asked about any other relatives being alive and I could only tell her about you.'

'I'm not a blood relative,' said Amelia.

'That's just what the woman said, but I took the name down just in case. It's Baskerville, miss, Jane Baskerville. That name ring a bell at all with you, miss?'

'Never heard of her,' said Amelia cheerfully, 'but I dare say I shall. Mr Morton, I'm going over to Great Primer presently with my stepmother and I'll be in touch with you later . . .'

'Right you are, miss. Keep left by the church and you're practically there but I don't think you and Dr Phoebe will have any difficulty finding the Grange.'

They didn't.

Amelia was aware of a strange sensation of unease, though, as they walked up to the old house. Dismissing it as a compound of curiosity and sudden responsibility she set the key of the Grange into the big old-fashioned lock of the front door.

That barely identified feeling was swiftly succeeded by

a very much more definite and devastating one as the two women stepped over the threshold.

The house had been ransacked.

SIX

Bird, beast, and goldfish are sepulchred there.

'Looks to me, sir,' said Detective Constable Crosby profoundly, after he had set eyes on the interior of the Grange, 'like a game of Hunt the Thimble turned nasty. Very nasty.'

He had just delivered his superior officer to the village of Great Primer at a speed that in any other circumstances would have rightly been deemed deplorable.

Detective Inspector Sloan was still getting his breath back and listening to Amelia Kennerley at the same time.

'I don't know who did it or what they were looking for, Inspector,' she said steadily, 'but they certainly made a good job of it.'

'Seems that they could have had all the time in the world anyway,' murmured Dr Phoebe Plantin, 'if Mortons' removed the body yesterday morning.'

Amelia immediately protested: 'But Phoebe, that would mean that whoever did all this knew straightaway that Great-Aunt Octavia had died when she did . . .' Her voice fell away and she looked uncertainly at Sloan. 'Doesn't it?'

'It looks as if someone knew, all right, miss,' said Sloan, regarding the havoc of books and paper strewn everywhere, 'although we can't say exactly when they knew. Or even if they did know, come to that. Not yet, we can't.'

'And it also looks as if they knew what they were

looking for, too,' remarked Dr Plantin gruffly. 'See over there, Inspector, on that sideboard . . .'

Sloan switched his gaze to follow her pointing finger.

'They didn't touch those Dresden shepherd-girls and you can take it from me that they're worth a bomb.'

'It rather seems,' observed Detective Inspector Sloan cautiously, 'as if they might have been in search of the written word.'

'It must have been a very comprehensive search,' murmured Amelia, finding just the right adjective for what she was looking at with difficulty. 'Come through here, Inspector . . .'

The chaos in what was obviously a combined library and study was indescribable.

'It looks,' said Amelia, 'as if every single book in the room has been taken off its shelf, thoroughly shaken and then dropped on the floor . . . and as for that . . .'

She pointed at a fine burr-walnut bureau which stood open, its drawers upturned and empty on the floor.

'It wasn't locked so it's probably not badly damaged,' said the policeman with a wisdom born out of years of experience. 'No, don't touch it, miss. Don't anyone touch anything. Crosby, get a scenes of crime officer out here and the photograph people – Dyson and Williams if they're free.' He stood for a long moment on the threshold of the library, gazing at the scene of chaos before him.

Amelia shivered at his side and said: 'It wasn't an ordinary burglary, was it, Inspector?'

Sloan shook his head. 'And it wasn't an ordinary search either, miss. Now, if you two ladies will just wait here, my constable and I will take a quick look round upstairs.'

He didn't know how old the house was but it was big and comfortable and there was an old-fashioned pre-war opulence about its fixtures and fittings that had never come back after August 1914. The staircase was wide and

45

the treads deep and the banister had been crafted out of cedarwood and was well polished for this day and age. The two policemen mounted it carefully, mindful of the possibility of the impression of footprints on the thick Turkey carpet.

Sloan sent Crosby to examine all the lesser rooms while he himself made for what the house agents call the master bedroom. He was not unbearably surprised to see the disturbance of the library replicated there.

Some person or persons at the moment unknown would seem to have been looking very hard indeed for something. The degree of devastation was so wide as to suggest that the search had failed. With luck, time would tell whether or not this was so.

Time and hard work.

Not forgetting luck, though.

If there was one thing which Sloan had learned over the years it was that you should never underestimate the element of luck in detective work.

Whoever had been conducting the search of the Grange hadn't scrupled to heap the contents of the bedroom drawers on to the bed so recently occupied by a dead woman. Here was no ceremonial *lit de mort* but a stripped bed, the mattress ticking covered with a single sheet, but otherwise bare.

To begin with Sloan stood just inside the doorway, letting his first impressions sink in. A medical oxygen bottle, mask still dangling from the knobs, stood to the far side of the head of the bed. On the side nearer the door, standing on a little cabinet that William Morris himself might have designed, was a telephone and two bottles of tablets, both nearly full.

Whoever had been in the room, then, since Mrs Garamond's death, had either not been concerned with removing her medication or had wished it to be seen and examined.

Examined it would be, he decided, shifting his gaze to the bed itself. It was a double one, with a second bedside cabinet at the further side. Also on the far side was a bed-light. It was of the movable vintage that sat on the bed-head, a pull-cord hanging down from it. On a tallboy beyond the bed had clearly been a small selection of books between ornamental book-ends. Books and book-ends were now all scattered on the bedroom floor.

Sloan stooped and tried to read a title or two without touching anything. Bedroom books, he reminded himself, were the books a person usually read – Gault and Synge's *Dictionary of Roses* lived by his own pillow – and he was beginning to be very curious indeed about what sort of a person the late Mrs Octavia Garamond had been.

Educated, he decided at once.

Widely educated, he decided a few moments later, having found one of the works of Sigmund Freud on the carpet cheek by jowl with Fyodor Dostoevsky's *Crime and Punishment*. Sloan himself, when an aspiring young constable, had – like many another – been drawn by the title. It had seemed almost required reading for a budding policeman but he had soon taken the book back to the public library. There had been no more connection between crime and punishment in the novel than there was in real life . . .

'Ain't nobody about, sir, but us chickens,' said Crosby, 'though all the other bedrooms are in pretty much the same state as this one.'

'Upside-down?' It was a calculated understatement.

'And how! Whatever it was they wanted, sir, they sure wanted it pretty badly.'

'And,' observed Sloan, moving carefully in the direction of the fireplace, 'we don't even know whether they found it, do we?'

'No, sir.' Crosby squinted down at the floor. 'Funny book-ends . . .'

Sloan took another look. They still seemed vaguely ornamental to him. Metal but stylish.

'Made from shrapnel,' said Crosby confidently. 'There's a chap with a shop down by the market who still sells that sort of thing. Undertones of War, he calls himself.'

Sloan peered more closely. 'So they are.' He started to study the photographs on the mantelpiece. They were all in silver frames but did not seem to have interested the searcher since they appeared quite undisturbed. In the centre was an amateur snapshot of a tall, laughing girl, her hair swept back from a fine face. One hand was waving gaily at whoever had been taking the photograph, the other engaged in holding her coat together in a high wind.

'That the girl downstairs, then?' asked Crosby over his shoulder.

'Not in that style of coat,' said Sloan. 'But there's a family likeness, I'll grant you that . . .' The next two photographs were of a man taken decades apart but pipe-smoking in both.

'Youth and age,' commented Crosby. 'Wore quite well, didn't he?'

'And here, Crosby, at a guess, is where the shrapnel came from.' He pointed to a picture of a large factory building covered in camouflage paint, with three rows of staff standing and sitting outside. There was an inscription in the bottom right-hand corner, which read *Chernwoods' Dyestuffs, May 8th, 1945.*

The day peace broke out.

In Europe, that is.

For the time being, anyway.

'Chernwoods' doesn't look like that now,' said Crosby. 'I passed it last week.'

'It isn't covered with camouflage paint any longer, that's why.' Sloan searched the faces in the photograph carefully until he found the one he wanted – it was half-way along the middle row. 'And they've repaired the bomb damage.'

He knew the building well enough as it was now. Chernwoods' Dyestuffs was still one of the biggest employers in Luston, which was Calleshire's only really large industrial town. Sloan turned back to the door with the distinct feeling that his mind had failed to register something significant. He would have to come back again later, although he knew for a start that there would be no point in examining the back of the wardrobe, now or then. Anyone ever searching a woman's bedroom always went straight to her wardrobe first.

And with good reason.

Especially if the woman was a drinker.

Instead, Sloan bent down and had a look at the jumble of books on the floor.

There was no Bible.

He would have expected to have found a Bible. His own mother always had one at her bedside. Old ladies in chronic heart failure usually had a Bible by their beds. And inside their Bible was where they often kept their really precious mementoes.

He looked on the floor and beside the bed again.

There was definitely no Bible.

Sloan and Crosby were half-way down the stairs when they heard the telephone bell ring.

Amelia Kennerley picked up the receiver in the hall and said: 'Hullo . . .'

'Great Primer Grange?' enquired a male voice. 'The late Mrs Garamond's house?'

'Yes,' said Amelia, conscious that everyone in the Grange was watching her face. 'Who is that speaking, please?'

'My name is Gregory Rosart. I'm from Chernwoods' Dyestuffs in Luston . . .' There was nothing in his voice,

49

decided Amelia, to convey the man. 'I do apologize for troubling you so soon and on a Saturday afternoon, too, but I've just seen the announcement in this morning's newspaper. We're all naturally very sorry to learn of Mrs Garamond's death . . .'

'How kind of you to ring,' said Amelia.

'But,' went on the voice fluently, 'I'm the firm's librarian and information officer and I'm ringing to say how very much we at Chernwoods' would appreciate a sight of Mrs Garamond's papers – she and her husband used to work here, you know, during the war – and we'd also very much like the opportunity to purchase any documents that there may be for our archives . . .'

Amelia gave a sudden high and humourless laugh. 'I'm sorry, Mr Rosart, but you haven't been quite quick enough off the mark.'

'But . . .'

'Saturday or not,' she declared, very conscious that she was being watched by two policemen and her stepmother, 'I'm afraid someone else has already had first pickings.'

'What!' exclaimed the voice. 'How did tha—'

'Without asking,' said Amelia astringently.

Gregory Rosart let out a low whistle. 'That was quick . . .'

SEVEN

Bid the black kitten march as chief mourner,

Gregory Rosart lost no time in calling on Joe Keen, the chief chemist of Chernwoods' Dyestuffs, Ltd., in person. He drove swiftly out to Joe's home in Larking. The house there, set in its own mellow grounds, was a far cry from the grimy building in Luston where both men worked. There was no doubt, thought Rosart, looking round him, that the Keen family home had that certain something called style.

Joe Keen took some pride in being a man of few words. He heard Rosart out and then said: 'And?'

'And,' said Rosart, 'we still don't know how much Harris and Marsh have really got hold of.'

'Enough to make them go on buying, anyway,' said Keen. 'They picked up another sizeable tranche of Chernwoods' 25p Ordinary Voting Shares late yesterday afternoon.'

'Good timing, that,' said Rosart appreciatively. 'You can't teach 'em much.'

'Just before the Stock Exchange closed for the weekend,' nodded Keen. 'Neat, wasn't it?'

'Our Claude won't have got a lot of sleep then . . .'

The chief chemist said: 'It frightened the life out of him.'

Claude Miller, Chairman and Managing Director of Chernwoods' Dyestuffs, was a living exemplification of the old saw about it being 'only three generations from clogs to clogs'. His father hadn't been the man his grand-father was and, worse still, Claude Miller wasn't even the man his father had been.

'I'll bet it did,' grinned Rosart. 'What we still don't know though,' he went on more urgently, 'is whether Harris and Marsh have got it or not.'

'That's true, Greg,' Keen gave a thin smile, 'but I think we soon will.'

'How come?'

'Because I reckon Harris and Marsh'll take the pressure off Chernwoods' just as soon as they have. I bet you they'll want to stop buying the stock just as quickly as they can. After all, it's not that much of a bargain and God knows what they're using for money.'

'Credit,' said Rosart pithily. 'What you're really saying, Joe, is that if they've got what they want then they don't need us.' Rosart looked at the chief chemist and said: 'And then what?'

'Then it would become a slightly different ball-game, that's all.' Joe Keen was looking out of the window at the rural scenery but his mind was back in Luston. 'And then, Greg, only if what you call OZ is actually what Harris and Marsh's Chemicals is after.'

'But . . .'

'But we don't even know that for sure, do we?' Keen swung his gaze back into the room and fixed it on Greg Rosart.

'We do know, though, that they want us,' persisted Rosart, subconsciously bracing his shoulders. He never enjoyed it when Keen stared like that. 'And only us,' he reminded him.

And that was what was really important, added the librarian and information officer – but under his breath.

'And only now,' Keen put it. 'That's the most interest-ing development of all, isn't it?'

'True . . .'

'I think, Greg,' said Joe Keen profoundly, and rather pleased with his deliberate understatement, 'that we could call Harris and Marsh the unknown quantity in the equation.'

'So, miss,' Sloan said presently, 'we know that at least two other people called here at the Grange yesterday afternoon . . .'

'That's what Tod Morton told me, Inspector,' replied Amelia. 'The rector, Mr Fournier, who came to deliver a letter about the funeral service . . . hymns and things.'

'That's on the hall table,' interposed Dr Plantin. 'It was on the door-mat as we came in and I automatically picked it up and put it there. That was before I saw the rest of the house.'

'And a young woman called Jane Baskerville whom Mr Fournier saw while he was delivering his letter,' finished Amelia.

Sloan made a note of the names.

'We also know now,' said Amelia tightly, 'that Chernwoods' Dyestuffs wanted her papers, too.'

'Badly enough to ring here the very day they knew from the newspapers that she'd died,' said Phoebe Plantin, 'weekend or no. If that's how they did find out, of course,' she added shrewdly.

'We'll be calling on Chernwoods' in the course of our enquiries,' said Sloan formally. 'There's nothing else you can tell me, is there, miss?'

Amelia said slowly, 'Only that the undertaker told me that the rector didn't seem very willing to take my great-aunt's funeral but she had left instructions that he should.'

Policemen, pathologists, and information officers might all work on Saturdays and Sundays. Members of the legal profession, however, do not. It was Monday morning when Amelia kept her appointment with James Puckle in the solicitors' offices down by the bridge in Berebury.

'Miss Kennerley, do come in . . .' He waved her to a chair. 'All of this must have come as something of a surprise to you . . .'

Amelia considered the young solicitor before her and then said briefly, 'Yes.'

'The break-in must be a worry and I'm sorry that there had to be a post-mortem but in the circumstances . . .'

'Like Mary Tudor,' remarked Amelia.

'Mary Tudor?' James Puckle looked baffled.

'She was "dead and opened".'

'Oh, really? I didn't know . . . well, just like Mary Tudor, then.'

'Mary Tudor,' said Amelia bleakly, 'told them that they would find "Calais" engraved on her heart.'

'I understand that the results of the autopsy on your great-aunt are not yet available,' James Puckle opened a folder on his desk, 'although I know she had had heart trouble . . . er . . . too. However . . .'

'Yes?' Amelia's eye had been caught by James Puckle's tie. Blue with something crossed on it. Not swords, surely?

'I understand, Miss Kennerley, that you didn't know your great-aunt well?'

'Not at all,' she said with perfect truth.

The solicitor consulted a paper inside the folder. 'Even so, she seems prepared to place a great deal of trust in you.'

'It would appear,' said Amelia, matching his dry tone, 'that there isn't anyone else in the family left.'

'Perhaps . . . I mean, that may well be the case . . . exactly . . . perhaps that is so although we are not – how shall I put it? – absolutely certain about that yet.'

'If you don't count my father,' said Amelia.

'That relationship is even more tenuous than your own,' said James Puckle. 'Besides there is also the matter of your appearance.'

'My appearance? What on earth has that got to . . .'

'Apparently,' said James Puckle, looking her straight in the eye, 'you very much reminded our client of her deceased daughter, Perpetua.'

Amelia, slightly startled, said: 'You seem to know quite a lot about me, Mr Puckle.'

The solicitor said: 'We took steps to find out what we could on our client's behalf when we established exactly what it was that Mrs Garamond wanted you to do.'

'Which is?'

'Mrs Garamond,' he responded obliquely, 'for reasons best known to herself chose to express her testamentary wishes in the form of some precatory words . . .'

'And what,' asked Amelia immediately, 'might precatory words be?'

'Words of wish, hope, desire, or entreaty,' responded the solicitor.

'I see . . .' She didn't see anything.

'Usually accompanying a gift with the intention that the recipient will dispose of the property in a particular way.'

Light began to dawn on Amelia. 'Great-Aunt Octavia wanted something doing?'

'I think you might put it like that,' said the solicitor.

'Something – this thing that she wants me to do – is it something that she couldn't do herself?'

'I think that is a fair inference.' He hesitated. 'Unless, that is, she had tried to do it herself and failed. We don't know about that.'

'To do what?' asked Amelia.

'Find someone.'

'Who?'

'Ah, there we have a slight difficulty.' James Puckle indicated a piece of paper in his hand. 'She wants you to find a woman who would be in her fifties now but . . .'

'But?' Amelia had managed to have a closer look at the design on the solicitor's tie. It wasn't crossed swords that she had been looking at but crossed hockey sticks. And the crest of the Berebury Hockey Club.

'I'm afraid,' said Puckle regretfully, 'that Mrs Garamond had no idea of the name this woman might be using at the time of her death.'

'That does rather widen the field,' agreed Amelia gravely, 'doesn't it?'

'It is part of the difficulty,' said James Puckle. 'Only part, though.'

She sat back in her chair. 'Tell me . . .'

'Once found, if she can be found, there is this precatory trust which Mrs Garamond created in her Will with which you will have to deal.'

Amelia stared at him. 'This woman – what does – did – my great-aunt know about her, then? If I'm to find her I shall need to . . .'

'The name of her mother and when she was born . . .' responded James Puckle.

'And where?' put in Amelia astringently.

'And where,' agreed the solicitor. 'I have her birth certificate in my file here . . .'

'And?' said Amelia into the little silence that fell when he stopped speaking.

'That would appear to be the extent of my client's knowledge,' said Puckle gently, 'at the time when she made her Will, that is.'

Amelia stared at him. 'That's all?'

James Puckle reached inside the folder. 'You were to be given this photograph, though.'

Amelia put out her hand in silence.

'I fear it is not a photograph of the person concerned,' he said, handing it to her across the desk.

'But I should be grateful for small mercies? Is that what you think?' Actually it was more of a snapshot than a proper photograph, and a little blurred at that. It was in black and white, quite small and rather faded, too. It appeared to Amelia to be of a wayside memorial beside a country crossroads. She peered at the image carefully. 'A memorial cross but not in a cemetery?'

'Not a grave,' agreed Puckle. 'I think there is an inscription but it's too small to read even with my grandfather's magnifying glass.'

Amelia screwed up her eyes but couldn't read it either.

'It looked to me,' the solicitor said, 'as if it's at a road junction, but where – I couldn't begin to say.'

'In France, anyway,' said Amelia promptly.

'France?'

'In Flanders fields, Mr Puckle, where poppies grow.' Amelia regarded the solicitor across the tooled green leather-topped expanse of his partners' desk and said: 'You're not pulling my leg about all this, are you, Mr Puckle?'

'Oh, no, Miss Kennerley, indeed not, I do assure you. Quite the contrary, in fact. The matter is serious. Very serious indeed.'

'I would say that whoever broke into the Grange was pretty serious, too.' said Amelia. 'Do you think that the two things are connected?'

James Puckle frowned. 'I can't answer that. I can only say that my instructions were that you were to be given the key of the Grange as well as the birth certificate and the photograph.' He straightened his tie and said, 'It is possible that there is a great deal of money waiting for this woman if she can be found.'

'Possible?' Amelia said. 'What exactly do you mean by possible?'

James Puckle said: 'Let me first of all explain to you the nature of a precatory trust.'

'It might help,' said Amelia, taking the tie-straightening as a sign of more to come. 'On the other hand, it might not.'

He gave a quick smile. 'It is usually used as a legal

57

device by which a man could arrange for the discreet support of a mistress, and any family which he has had by her, after he had died without his wife and the rest of his family needing to learn of their existence.'

'I should have thought,' rejoined Amelia militantly, 'that any wife worth her salt would have guessed.'

James Puckle did not rise to this but went on: 'Precatory settlements were most commonly used in Victorian times . . .'

'When the Queen would not have been amused . . .'

'When there was a greater opprobrium attached to . . . er . . . irregular liaisons.'

'Are you trying to tell me,' demanded Amelia forthrightly, 'that my great-aunt had a toy-boy?'

'I'm trying to tell you about precatory trusts and settlements,' said James Puckle mildly.

'Oh, all right. Go on.'

'The mechanism behind the device is really quite simple . . .'

'Simple! Oh, sorry . . .'

'The testator would leave an appropriate sum of money to his best friend or someone else whom he could trust . . .'

'Best friends don't always have a good track record for trustworthiness.'

'True. Nevertheless the testator would select a friend or member of his family . . .'

'Not always one and the same either.'

'In whom he felt he could repose his trust and make them legatees – often residuary legatees as this was more flexible and then . . .' James Puckle paused.

'And then . . .?' prompted Amelia, leaning forward in her chair now.

'And then arrange for them to be handed a sealed envelope with the Will in which the testator would explain that the money that they had been left was not actually for them at all but for the secret upkeep of the mistress.'

Amelia sat back and said: 'I really don't see what this has got to do with me.'

'Quite a lot, Miss Kennerley. You must appreciate that Mrs Garamond has made you her sole executrix and her residuary legatee on the understanding – the unwritten and discreet understanding as far as the Will is concerned, mind you – that you first find this woman . . .'

'And then?' said Amelia tautly.

'Mrs Garamond's instructions require that, once found, a judgement must be made before the bulk of her estate is handed over to her.'

'But . . .'

'A very subjective judgement about her worthiness to inherit.'

Amelia took a deep breath. 'So I'm to be both judge and jury, am I? Always supposing that we can find her in the first place . . .'

'The precatory trust gives you total discretion.' James Puckle rustled his papers. 'However, should your actions be challenged at any time – although I can't imagine by whom – then, of course, we would be very happy to act for you.'

Amelia wrinkled her brow in puzzlement. 'And if I don't – if I can't – find her, or even if she's dead – then what?'

'The residue of your great-aunt's estate remains yours.'

Amelia said wryly: 'Keeping it in the family, I suppose?'

'Just so, Miss Kennerley,' said the solicitor. 'The connection is there. Your late mother and the testator's daughter, Perpetua, were first cousins after all.'

Amelia nodded her concurrence with this statement. Puckle, Puckle, and Nunnery had really done their homework on her background.

James Puckle was still going on. 'The precatory words,

I must remind you, are merely a private wish, hope, desire . . .'

'And entreaty,' she finished for him.

'Expressed in writing in private.' He coughed. 'I must remind you that no Trust within the legal meaning of the term is actually established although under more recent legislation it is possible that she might have a separate claim in her own right . . .'

Amelia was scarcely listening now. Her mind had wandered back to the odd disturbance at the Grange: it might be even more important now.

'And that the provisions of neither the various Trust Acts nor those of the precatory words are legally enforceable.' He looked at her and asked, 'Do I make myself quite clear?'

'Like Charles II saying, "Let not poor Nellie starve"?' said Amelia.

'Just like King Charles, Miss Kennerley, except,' he said drily, 'that you may wish to take more note of what your great-aunt wanted than the King's friends and relations did. I understand that, in fact, King Charles' poor Nellie did starve.'

'And if I don't?' asked Amelia curiously.

'That,' said the solicitor, 'is a matter entirely between you and your conscience.'

'I see.'

'I must also advise you that you can, of course, decline to act at all if you so wish.'

'It being a free country.' Amelia looked James Puckle straight in the eye and said: 'Do we know why Great-Aunt Octavia left her money in this way to a woman whose name she didn't know and I mustn't mention?'

'Oh, yes, Miss Kennerley,' responded the solicitor. 'That's no problem. You see, she was her daughter.'

'But her daughter Perpetua died . . .'

'Not Perpetua,' James Puckle said. 'She had had another baby before she married your mother's uncle . . .'

EIGHT

Weaving her tail like a plume in the air

'And Phoebe,' Amelia gulped, laying a copy of the birth certificate which James Puckle had given her on the kitchen table for her stepmother to see, 'do you know, Great-Aunt Octavia's left a pathetic message for me to give to her daughter when – if – I find her. And in her Will she's left a candle – that's all – for someone called Kate. Isn't it all so sad?'

Dr Plantin nodded.

'To think she's wanted to see her so badly all those years . . .' said Amelia.

Phoebe Plantin plonked her large lady doctor's hand-bag firmly on the kitchen floor, pulled up a chair to the table, and examined the document. 'A female child,' she read aloud, 'born December 15th, 1940. Mother's sur-name Harquil-Grasset . . .'

'Go on,' urged Amelia.

'Father unknown,' said Phoebe.

'When I find her,' said Amelia a little unsteadily, 'I'm to tell her how sorry she was to have inflicted the tache – James Puckle says that's an old Scots word meaning mark – the tache of bastardy on her but she only did what she thought was right at the time.'

'Nobody can do more,' commented Phoebe Plantin sagely. 'I don't know about her surname but she gave her enough Christian names, didn't she?'

'Erica Hester Goudy,' quoted Amelia. 'I know, but James Puckle says she might not have kept them when she was adopted She's just as likely to be called something like Mary Smith now.'

'Born in a nursing home in London,' observed Dr Plantin, still regarding the birth certificate minutely, 'and while there was a war on.'

'She probably told them she was a war widow,' said Amelia.

'Shouldn't be surprised,' said Phoebe Plantin, who had ceased to be surprised long ago. 'And arranged for flowers to be sent to herself, I expect. It's been done before. Not that that sort of nursing home would ask questions, anyway.'

'But, look,' Amelia pointed at a line on the birth certificate, 'she did put her own occupation down.'

'Biological chemist . . .' said the older woman thoughtfully. 'She must have been pretty bright to go in for that before the last war.'

'She's left some money to her old college,' said Amelia. 'It's in the Will.'

'Thought of everything, hasn't she?'

'Anyway,' said Amelia, turning to give something on the stove her attention, 'it's all different now – having a baby adopted, I mean. Wasn't there an Act of Parliament or something whereby an adopted child can now find out about its real mother?'

'Indeed there was,' Phoebe Plantin said warmly, 'except that they never use the term real mother nowadays. You have to call her the birth mother instead . . .'

'But what about the new law?' Amelia wished she'd paid more attention in her civics class at school – law seemed a very remote subject when viewed from the perspective of the sixth form. 'What was that about, then?'

'The Children's Act of 1975 is the one you mean, but,' Phoebe shook her head – 'it isn't going to help you find Octavia Garamond's daughter, I'm afraid.'

Amelia turned away from the stove. 'Why not?'

'Because while the Act gave children who had been adopted the right to find out about their birth mothers when they reached the age of eighteen,' said her step-mother, 'it didn't give their birth mothers any right to find out what had become of their natural children who had been adopted . . .'

'But . . .'

'What you might call sauce for the goslings but not for the goose.'

'Or gander?'

'Or gander,' said Phoebe Plantin, tapping the birth certificate. 'When Erica Hester Goudy Harquil-Grasset was adopted, which is presumably what happened to her since her birth mother couldn't trace her later . . .'

'If she tried,' said Amelia. 'We don't even know that.'

'She would have been given a new birth certificate.'

'I can see that,' said Amelia, 'but . . .'

'The Registrar General keeps a confidential record of adoptions and the connection between the old and the new names to which only the child has access,' said Dr Plantin, adding authoritatively: 'and then only after he or she has reached the age of eighteen and has been professionally counselled.'

'Not the real – sorry – birth mother?'

'Not the birth mother,' said Dr Plantin.

'But there's nothing, surely, to stop her trying to find out, is there?' asked Amelia, stirring the while. 'It's a free country . . .'

'Nothing.' Phoebe Plantin pushed the birth certificate to one side and took up her table napkin. 'But there are only two things that she can do which are really helpful.'

'Which are?'

'One is to deposit her name and address with the Registrar saying that she is willing for it to be given to her child should he or she ever try to seek to find out its mother's identity, and indicating that she wishes to make contact with the child so that if the child wishes it can go straight ahead.'

'And the other?' asked Amelia.

'Advertise. You've probably seen advertisements asking for an adopted child born on such and such a date to write to someone who may be its mother,' said Dr Plantin. 'It's open to abuse on both sides of course, but you might have to do something like that.'

'Or,' said Amelia, 'follow up every female child born on December 15th, 1940.'

'Difficult,' said Phoebe Plantin placidly. 'Even Herod had his problems in that direction for all that he was King.'

'King Herod?'

'He tried, didn't he? And if that's soup on the stove, it's burning.'

'Ah, Sloan . . .' Superintendent Leeyes could usually be found sitting in his office very much as a spider saves her strength and keeps watch on her web. The only real difference was that while the spider has to wait for her victim to get entangled in her net, the superintendent sent for his.

'Sir?'

'There you are, at last . . .' The superintendent had long ago raised the wrong-footing of his subordinates to a fine art. 'This Garamond business . . . you're making progress, I hope?'

'We've established that whoever did the damage at Great Primer Grange got in through a pantry window at the back of the house' – Sloan wasn't sure if this was exactly progress or not and pressed on – 'at some time as yet unknown after Mortons', the undertakers, removed the body during Friday morning, and before Miss Kennerley and Dr Plantin went in on Saturday afternoon.'

'You wouldn't care to narrow that down at all, would

you, Sloan?' asked Leeyes with mock solicitude. 'Say to Friday or Saturday or when there's an "R" in the month?'

'Not at the moment, sir, thank you.' He consulted his notebook and went on: 'We have also established that the intruder or intruders wore gloves . . .'

'So what's new?' shrugged Leeyes.

'The fact,' replied Sloan literally, 'that they also wore some sort of overshoe – presumably to blur any footprints that might have been left. The carpets at the Grange are very good ones.'

Leeyes grunted.

'Whether the young woman who was seen by the local rector leaving the premises at half-past four on Friday afternoon had a hand in the break-in we have yet to find out,' went on Sloan. 'The name she gave and a rough description have been circulated . . . and DC Crosby is out interviewing the woman who was on duty as a care assistant at the Grange the night Mrs Garamond died.'

Leeyes grunted again.

'And then we're going over to Luston, sir. Both the Garamonds used to work at Chernwoods' Dyestuffs and the old firm . . .'

'Old firm nothing,' said Leeyes briskly. 'They were up in court last month for breaking the health and safety regulations and endangering the wellbeing of their work force. Didn't you notice?'

'Even so,' said Sloan, 'they seem to be taking quite an interest in the break-in at the Grange.'

'Do they?' growled Leeyes. 'Then make sure it's a healthy interest. Wait a minute, though, wait a minute, Sloan . . . there's someone else already taking an interest in Chernwoods' Dyestuffs, isn't there? It was in *The Chronicle*, surely, last week . . .'

'Harris and Marsh's Chemicals, sir,' supplied Sloan, who read the local newspaper too. 'I had a word with

"G" Division over at Luston about that this morning. Apparently Harris and Marsh've been trying for a take-over of Chernwoods' for quite a while now.'

'I always thought that dog doesn't eat dog,' objected Leeyes, 'but I suppose I'm old-fashioned.'

'If it's business, it does,' said Sloan without hesitation. 'That's not all, sir. The word in Luston is that rather than be – er – eaten by Harris and Marsh's Chemicals some of the senior people over at Chernwoods' Dyestuffs would go for a management buy-out.'

'Would they?' sniffed Leeyes. 'I suppose they know what they're doing, putting all their eggs in one basket like that.'

'It did occur to me, sir, to wonder if the deceased could have had a significant holding in Chernwoods', seeing as she and her husband both worked there once.'

'It wouldn't do any harm to find out,' conceded Leeyes.

'The deceased,' said Sloan, glancing down at his note-book again, 'would appear also to have had some profound disagreements in the past with the rector of Great Primer.'

'I do hope, Sloan,' said Leeyes irritably, 'that religion isn't going to come into all this. There'll be no holds barred then . . .'

As far as the chairman and managing director of Chernwoods' Dyestuffs was concerned there never had been any holds barred in business. This had been one of many of life's disappointments. He was now listening intently to Gregory Rosart's account of his telephone call to the Grange and feeling even more aggrieved.

'I thought I oughtn't to wait until today, Mr Miller, to try to establish contact,' said the press officer, carefully suppressing any mention of his visit to Joe Keen's. 'It might have been too late.'

Claude Miller gnawed the end of his knuckle. 'True.'

'And I was quite right. Someone had already been in there.'

'Beaten us to it, you mean, Greg?' said Miller. He liked to think he was good at facing up to the realities.

'Ah,' Rosart held up his finger, 'now that's something we don't really know yet, isn't it?'

'If you ask me,' said Claude Miller bitterly, 'that's the whole trouble. Nobody knows for sure how much of this business anyone else knows and we've got no way of finding out. It's all guesswork.'

'Now, I wouldn't say that, Mr Miller. Not yet . . .'

The care assistant who did the nights at the Grange was called Mrs Shirley Doves and made no bones about talking to a nice young police constable who seemed so interested in all her doings.

'Thursday night? Like every other night, it was. My Ron took me over from Cullingoak, 'bout half nine, it would be. I'd settle the kids – my mum pops in then to keep an eye – and then Ron brings me over to Great Primer.'

'So you'd get to the Grange when?' said Detective Constable Crosby. He knew he should be calling her 'madam' but he hadn't got it in him what it took to do it.

'Oh, we don't come straight to the Grange, lovey – I wasn't due there until half ten, you know. No, you see we pop into the Dog and Duck first. You know . . . the pub the other side of the church from the Grange. You must have seen it if you've been out there – call yourself a policeman and not know the pubs? Oh, all right, then . . . if you say so . . . My Ron knows the landlord, see . . . well, we go there first, otherwise,' Shirley laughed, 'I'd never see Ron at all, would I? Oh, all right, well hardly ever. You see, he's gone to work by the time I get back, mornings – my mum gets the kids off to school except the two littlest so this hour in the pub, evenings, is 'bout the only time we have together, Ron and me. Mind you,' she said elliptically, 'my mum says it's long enough when you've got four under six. She thinks it's time Ron shut up shop, anyway, but he doesn't like the idea.'

Detective Constable Crosby went a bit pink and asked if last Thurday night had been different in any way from other nights.

'Seeing as you ask,' admitted Shirley, 'I might have been a bit later than usual. Not much, mind you. You see, we got talking with a fellow there and he stood us an extra round just before we went. Not,' she went on hurriedly, 'that the old lady minded. I don't think she cared any more what time of day it was. 'Sides, she told me she was expecting a visitor the next afternoon. Quite excited about it, she was. Anyway, I settled her for the night like I always did, then I gave her a milky drink and her tablets, and went to bed myself. A bit early, actually. In the night? No, she didn't ring once and I slept right through, I did. Course, in the morning she'd gone, hadn't she? Not that that was any surprise to anyone. Could have happened any time, the doctor said. He's ever so nice, is Dr Aldus. He wasn't cross at all. He knew I wasn't meant to be sitting up with her or anything. Just there to see that she didn't come to no harm . . .'

NINE

Bury him nobly – next to the donkey

'Phoebe . . .'

'M'm?'

'I think,' said Amelia, 'that I'm going to need to know where Great-Aunt was for the whole of the year when her daughter was born.'

'So do I.'

'Tell me, if the baby was born on December 15th when would she have known that she was pregnant?'

Dr Plantin thought for a moment. 'In those days not until about the middle of May.'

'Those days?'

'Testing for pregnancy was different then.' She raised a minatory hand. 'I know, you're going to tell me that of course she would have known sooner, but you must remember that it wasn't like that then. Testing for pregnancy in 1940 took a long time and mice.'

'Mice?' echoed Amelia, surprised.

'Mice, rabbits, or frogs.' The telephone began to ring and Phoebe Plantin started to get to her feet. 'You could make a beginning by trying to find out, if you can, where your great-aunt was somewhere about the second half of March 1940.' She picked up her bag. 'That's when this baby would have been conceived. If that's my surgery on the phone tell them I'm on my way.'

'Phoebe, I'm not sure if I should have told you about the baby . . . she must have wanted it kept secret.'

70

'Mum's the word,' promised Dr Plantin as she left the room. She came back a moment later and said neatly, 'And in more senses than one.'

Amelia grinned and went to the telephone with Dr Plantin's message but the call was not for her stepmother but for her.

'Claude Miller here, Chairman of Chernwoods' Dyestuffs,' said a voice importantly. 'I'm ringing to say that I would count it a great privilege to be allowed to say something about Mrs Garamond at the funeral. Or, perhaps, read a lesson. I don't want to intrude, naturally, but, after all, she was connected with the firm here for a very long time.'

Amelia promised to talk to the rector. And then she did some dialling on her own behalf. 'Directory enquiries? I want the number of the bursar of Boleyn College please . . .'

The bursar had a high, thin voice and was called Miss Wotherspoon. 'In what way may I help you?' she piped. 'Who? Garamond, née Harquil-Grasset, did you say? Ah, yes, I saw that in the paper. Just a moment and I'll turn up our records . . .'

Amelia heard the patter of her footsteps across the floor and then their return.

'Are you there, Miss Kennerley? She came up as Brakewell Scholar before the war and read biological chemistry – we hadn't really started to call them biologists then – that word was only just beginning to come into fashion and Boleyn kept to the old style – Honours degree in Biological Chemistry.' Miss Wotherspoon drew breath and said: 'She did awfully well – awarded the Malthus Prize, Banksia Essayist for paper on mitosis in sugar beet . . . as it happened that was very useful afterwards—'

'Afterwards . . ?' broke in Amelia.

'No imported cane sugar to speak of in this country

71

after the war started – and I'm sure she'd have proceeded to a doctorate but for war breaking out . . . bound to have done.'

'Yes, of course,' said Amelia. 'That is certain to have made a difference.'

'Then did research at the Linnean Institute until 1940,' continued the bursar, obviously reading aloud, 'war-work at Messrs Chernwoods' Dyestuffs, Luston, Calleshire, married William Garamond 1941 . . .' Miss Wotherspoon's voice died away in patent disappointment. 'Only joint publications with William Garamond after that, I'm afraid. She doesn't seem to have published anything entirely on her own from then onwards . . .'

Amelia wondered briefly what Anne Boleyn would have made of this. Or Henry VIII.

'Always so difficult,' went on the bursar brightly, 'where you have joint papers with spouses to know who's done the real work but wives, even if they're very good, will do it. You can't stop them.'

'No,' said Amelia, 'but you will be very pleased to know that my great-aunt hasn't forgotten Boleyn in her Will . . .'

Detective Inspector Sloan had barely got back to his own office before his telephone went. It was the pathologist.

'She may have been murdered?' repeated Sloan.

'That's what I said and that's what I mean,' declared the pathologist unrepentantly. 'I've been talking to the people I sent those sections to.'

'And?'

'They're equivocal,' said Dr Dabbe, adding cheerfully, 'both the sections and the people.'

'But . . .'

'They're going to do some more tests but I thought meanwhile I ought to keep you in the picture.'

'Thank you, doctor, but . . .'

'If some noxious substance had been administered to the deceased,' swept on the pathologist, 'to account for the post-mortem findings in her liver and kidneys, then we don't yet know what it was.'

'When you say "administered", doctor, what precisely do you mean?'

'I mean,' said Dabbe easily, 'that it is not yet clear how the noxious substance got into the old lady's system – if it did, of course.'

'All her precautions,' said Sloan warily, 'seem to point to her having thought – er – malfeasance a possibility.'

'And all I can say at this stage,' said Dr Dabbe rather more informally, 'is that if someone was out to get her then they might have done . . .'

'But how?' said Sloan, with the classic trio of the prerequisites of murder, means, motive, and opportunity, in the forefront of his mind but left unsaid.

'Ah, that's another matter altogether,' said Dabbe. 'We can't tell you how just yet.'

'I see,' he said.

'I can tell you, though, some of the ways it wasn't,' said Dr Dabbe helpfully. 'She didn't swallow it because I took samples from her stomach, remember?'

Sloan remembered.

'And I also examined her body very carefully for puncture marks.'

'There weren't any.'

'Precisely, Sloan,' agreed the doctor. 'There weren't any. Like the curious incident of the dog in the night.'

'It didn't bark,' responded Sloan. Two could play at this game.

'That, as Sherlock Holmes remarked, was what was curious,' said the pathologist. 'Nor, I may say, were there any marks on her skin suggestive of the application of one of the transdermal poisons . . .'

'Pardon, doctor?'

'Hamlet's father . . .'

'The Ghost?'

'The Ghost, if you remember, Sloan, had been murdered by having a transdermal poison poured into his ear.'

'Mrs Garamond hadn't though, had she?' said Sloan, trying to keep his mind clear.

'Both ears,' responded Dabbe immediately, 'were dry and the drums visible, and neither John Aldus nor I found anything on her skin.'

'Yet she asked him to look,' said Sloan.

'So it would seem.'

'That leaves the nose . . .' said Detective Inspector Sloan, determined to remain undistracted by literary allusions. 'Could she have inhaled something?'

'I can't tell you that she didn't,' said the pathologist blandly. 'Not yet.'

'So where are we now, Crosby?'

'Just past the Calleford turn-off, sir.'

'Not where are we on the *road*, Crosby. I can see that for myself, thank you – if and when, that is, I can bring myself to open my eyes.'

'Sir?' Detective Constable Crosby sounded injured.

The two policemen were driving along Calleshire's only stretch of motorway, satisfying Crosby's lust for speed at the same time as seriously interfering with Sloan's digestive processes.

'I meant,' sighed Sloan, 'where have we got to in the case – if there is a case, that is – of the late Octavia Garamond?'

'Oh.' There was a long pause and then Crosby said tentatively: 'Not very far?'

'Surprise, surprise, Crosby. You could be right.'

'Thank you, sir.' A beam had replaced the injured look on the detective constable's face.

'All we've got so far might as well be called thistledown,' said Sloan. 'You could blow it away like a dandelion clock – what are you stopping for, Crosby? The road's quite clear . . .'

'Inspector Harpe of Traffic ordered a speed trap at the bottom of Bembo Hill today, sir.'

'Did he, indeed?' said Sloan. 'Good for him.'

'Yes, sir.' Crosby flashed the car's headlights at a uniformed constable wielding a hand-held computer-assisted radar gun as he drove past at his lowest speed of the week.

Sloan enjoyed a moment's relaxation. 'I shan't ask how you got to hear about it.'

'Thank you, sir.'

'But now that the immediate danger is over, Crosby, perhaps you would turn your mind to the matter on hand.'

'That,' advanced Crosby, 'was no ordinary turning-over at the Grange, sir.'

'No,' agreed Sloan.

'And whoever did it got started on the searching pretty quickly after the old lady died.'

'True.'

'And then there was her wanting her doctor to have a look at her after she'd died.'

'Good. Go on.'

'And asking us to the funeral.'

Sloan said very seriously, 'I think that there is no doubt that – whether or not she was – the deceased would seem to have thought that she might be murdered.'

'Seems to me,' said Crosby, resuming his usual speed, 'that she was pretty sure about it.'

'Either way,' said Sloan, 'since she was, from all accounts, a pretty bright old bird, I think her last wishes ought to be respected by everyone.'

'Then,' said Crosby, 'why didn't she tell someone about being afraid of being killed while she was still alive?'

'I've been thinking about this,' said Sloan, 'and I've come to the conclusion that she wasn't afraid of dying and didn't mind.'

Crosby took his foot off the accelerator in surprise. 'Not mind being murdered?'

'She was old, ill, and alone in the world, and her doctor agrees that she knew she hadn't long to live.'

Crosby put his foot down again.

Sloan said: 'I would think that she had already decided that she hadn't anything to live for . . .' He looked up and braced himself as they overtook a TVR sports car at a speed he didn't even like to think about. 'I would like you to know that I have, Crosby.'

'Sir?'

'Everything. A wife, a son, a pension, and now Madame Caroline Testout.'

'Sir?'

'An old Hybrid Tea rose. She's at her best just now.'

'Yes, sir.'

'And furthermore I would like you to know that I do not share your rooted objection to looking at the back view of the vehicle ahead.'

'Yes, sir.'

'Especially when I'm thinking about a very odd case where the pathologist and his cronies can't even be sure what the deceased died from.'

Detective Constable Crosby pulled the police car into the slow lane of the motorway just behind a heavily laden articulated lorry and trailer and said, 'This thing that someone was looking for at the Grange . . .'

'I agree it would help if we knew what it was . . .' Sloan responded to Crosby's thought processes rather than his words.

'Do you think, sir, that the old lady had it there? Whatever it was.'

'If she did,' said Sloan, 'then what I think is that she either knew it was there . . .'

'And that no one could find it?' said Crosby, edging the police car nearer still to the lorry's exhaust pipe.

'That,' said Detective Inspector Sloan, 'or, whether it was there or not, that she wanted them to come and show their hand.'

'Whoever they are?' said Crosby.

Sloan wound up the car window to keep the fumes out. 'Exactly. There was something else . . .'

'Sir?' Crosby peered through the cloud of smoke rather ostentatiously.

'Those notices about her death sent to all those different newspapers that Tod Morton told us about . . .'

'What about them, then?'

'I think that she was making absolutely sure that someone . . .'

'Person or persons unknown?' contributed Crosby, who was now rubbing the inside of the car's windscreen as if to disperse the lorry's effulgence.

'Knew that she'd died when she did.'

'So that they'd come and search her house?'

'Not exactly. They could have done that any time. From what Dr Aldus said Mrs Garamond would have been too frail to stop them.'

'So, what then, sir?'

'So that they'd come and search her house after she was dead. There is quite a difference.'

It was too fine a point for Crosby. He concentrated on pulling the police car out into the fast lane instead.

They were very nearly into Luston before he spoke again. 'Sir, how are we ever going to know if they—'

'Person or persons unknown?'

'Them,' said the constable, 'got what it was they wanted or not?'

'Ah! Now you're asking,' said Sloan.

TEN

Fetch the old banner, and wave it about;

Exactly the same problem was worrying Michael Harris of Messrs Harris and Marsh's Chemicals, also of Luston. He found it as difficult a question to answer as Detective Inspector Sloan had done.

Unlike Sloan and Gregory Rosart, though, Michael Harris had no one with whom he could talk completely freely on that particular matter. He was, however, able to discuss his predatory stalking of Chernwoods' Dyestuffs with his finance director – indeed, he had to talk to David Gillsans because some of the fine print of the rules and regulations appertaining to take-over deals of limited companies still evaded him. Like his father before him, Michael Harris was primarily a chemist and not either a legal eagle or a money man. He looked to his finance director, David Gillsans, to be both.

'So what do we hold of Chernwoods' now, David?' Harris asked him first thing Monday morning.

'As of stock-market closing time last Friday afternoon, just one per cent under the percentage when we would have to go public on the bid.'

'That's not including my father's own holding, is it?'

'No,' said the finance director patiently. This was old ground and they'd been over it before.

'Or Octavia Garamond's?'

'Naturally not.'

'She died on Friday.'

'So I saw in the newspaper.'

'What happens to her holding now?'

'That depends on how she willed it. If she didn't specify the shares in her Will as a bequest then her executors may choose to sell to raise funds for capital transfer and inheritance tax . . .'

'I wish you'd call it by its proper name, David,' said Harris snappily, 'then at least I would know what you were talking about . . .'

'Death duties,' said David Gillsans smoothly. He toyed momentarily with the idea of telling his employer that the tax had its early origins as a fine on a subject for dying and thus depriving the Crown of the services of the deceased – but decided against it. Harris was all on edge enough this morning as it was. He said instead, 'There'll be a bit of a delay of course before they can be sold – probate and so forth. Solicitors never hurry.'

'She'll have had a big holding,' Harris mused, 'because there were two of them, then. Her and her husband.'

'It's difficult to remember that Chernwoods' Dyestuffs must have been in quite a bad way after the war,' said David Gillsans peaceably, 'and needing capital.' This was much safer ground. Michael Harris was always ready to recount how his own father and Freddie Marsh had walked away from Chernwoods' after the last war and set up their own firm on the other side of town: and how Albert Harris had kept his Chernwoods' shares, too, so that he could keep an eye on how their nearest rival was doing. Not that balance sheets said everything. Old Albert Harris'd known that much before he and Freddie Marsh had branched out on their own.

'Must have been hard going for all of them then,' said Michael Harris. 'Mind you, I was no'but a boy myself at the time but Dad talked about it a lot at home.'

'Did they part brass rags?' asked David Gillsans curiously. 'I mean, did your father and Freddie have a row or just walk out on them?'

'Oh, no, nothing like that,' responded Harris, sensing

criticism. 'The Garamonds were able to put real money into Chernwoods', you see, and Dad and Freddie couldn't. Not at the time. Dad just had a few shares for old times' sake and to see how they were doing.'

'And how is your father?' enquired David Gillsans politely. Freddie Marsh had died long ago.

'Much as usual,' shrugged Harris. 'Rambling, like he always does these days. I'm not even sure that he knows me now.'

'Pity, when you think of what he did in the past.' David Gillsans would not have dreamed of saying that he thought it just as well that Harris's father didn't know what was going on. The old man would never have agreed to this ill-advised take-over battle that his son was bent on.

Hell-bent, amended Gillsans silently.

Fortunately Harris was no mind-reader. He went on: 'I sat by his bed most of Sunday afternoon – not that it does any good. Still it's just as well to take an interest or the nursing home gets slack.'

'Very true,' nodded Gillsans.

'Sad when you think of him as he was.'

'Indeed.' As it happened, the finance director knew a great deal about the early struggles of Harris and Marsh's Chemicals Ltd., since he not only had access to the old company reports and balance sheets but could understand them as well. Old Albert Harris had done well in his day – and had a bit of luck, too, when he had needed it.

As always, Michael Harris came back to his own consuming passion to take over Chernwoods' Dyestuffs.

'He'd be very pleased, David, if he knew what we were doing now. It was his dream, too, you know, to end up owning the firm where he first worked.'

The finance director remained unmoved by his employer's dreams: in his view personalities shouldn't be allowed to affect financial decisions. 'There's no sentiment in business,' he warned.

'You tell that to Chernwoods' when we get 'em in our net.'

'If we get them,' Gillsans reminded his boss, not for the first time. In the accountant's book, schoolboy rivalries should not outlive the playground. 'It's not in the bag yet, remember.'

'If the law doesn't say you can't,' said Michael Harris gnomically, 'then you can.' Just then the door of his office was opened after a perfunctory tap and his secretary came in. He looked round. 'Yes, Deanne, what is it?'

'It's my cousin Doreen on the switchboard down at Chernwoods', Mr Harris . . .'

'Yes?' Michael Harris sprang to attention much as those at Ghent might have done when the messenger arrived from Aix.

'She says they've got the police round there,' reported Deanne, wide eyed.

ELEVEN

Bury him deeply – think of the monkey,

Luston was Calleshire's principal industrial town. As English settlements went it was old enough in its history to match Berebury itself – even Calleford – but it hadn't burgeoned into a real town until the middle of the nineteenth century, when, with the advent of the railway, it had suddenly started to grow.

Claude Miller, Chairman of the Board and Chief Executive of Chernwoods' Dyestuffs, received Detective Inspector Sloan and Detective Constable Crosby with a judiciously balanced blend of courtesy and curiosity. Gregory Rosart, information officer and librarian, was at his side. Miller, noted Sloan, was a tall, rangy figure, thin as a yard of rainwater, and given to unnecessary jerky movements, while Rosart was short and thick-set, with fat, puffy hands.

Miller said: 'I've had Greg here dig out the records you asked for, Inspector.'

'Mrs Garamond came to the firm early in 1941, Inspector,' contributed Rosart fluently. 'She was just Miss O. L. A. Harquil-Grasset, B.Sc., in those days, by the way. She didn't marry until later.'

'I understand,' supplemented Claude Miller, 'that she was one of our best people at the time . . .'

'The notes I've turned up,' chimed in the information officer, 'describe her as a very promising young scientist . . .'

'And,' enquired Sloan pertinently, 'was that early promise fulfilled?' There were men who had been at the Police Training College with him who were rising chief constables now . . . and other men who had been there then who were still constables acting as human traffic lights in the constabulary equivalent of a punishment station.

'Oh, yes, indeed.' It was Claude Miller who responded this time. 'What work she did in the war is mostly still covered by the Official Secrets Act and we don't have complete records, naturally . . .'

'Naturally,' concurred the detective inspector, who had taken – and kept – his own Oath of Loyalty.

'But afterwards she and her husband – as you know she later married William Garamond, who also worked here – he was a pure chemist . . .'

Detective Inspector Sloan made an *aide memoire* in his notebook. He saw no point in trying to guess what a pure chemist was. Or in trying to tell the superintendent until he knew for certain.

'Well,' said Claude Miller impressively, sounding like the decisive chairman of the board that he would like to have been, 'they were among those whose work made Chernwoods' Dyestuffs what it is today.'

'And what is it today?' enquired Detective Inspector Sloan. He saw no reason to mention that he had already dispatched an urgent request to Companies' House for the fullest of details of not only Chernwoods' Dyestuffs but of Harris and Marsh's Chemicals as well.

Oddly enough the chairman of the board of Chernwoods' left the answering of this question to his information officer. 'One of the more important smaller companies in the bio-chemical medical-research sector, gentlemen,' recited Gregory Rosart unhesitatingly.

'Where do the dyestuffs come in then?'

'Ah, Inspector,' continued Rosart, after a quick glance

at his chairman, 'that has its origins in our early history. Chernwoods' Dyestuffs first began about a hundred and fifty years ago as a processor of natural dyes – both *Isatis tinctoria* and *Reseda luteola* grew naturally in these parts . . .'

'And are you going to tell me what they are?' asked Detective Inspector Sloan, who didn't like being talked down to any more than did the next man.

'Waxen woad and dyer's weld,' said Rosart. Claude Miller's attention seemed to be elsewhere.

'I see,' said Sloan, nodding. He thought about the photograph on the bedroom mantelpiece at the Grange and said: 'And in the war?'

He was immediately aware of a stiffening on Miller's part, while there was a barely perceptible tenseness in Gregory Rosart's posture, too subtle to be described as a bracing but a change in manner for all that.

'According to my research, Inspector,' said Rosart, 'Chernwoods' went over to war-work in September 1939.'

'Before my time,' said Claude Miller lightly. 'I've only been with the firm since my father died about ten years ago. He and my grandfather would have been able to help you more.'

'And did what,' persisted Sloan, keeping his eye on the ball, 'in the war?'

'A great many things,' said Rosart.

'Chemical warfare work?'

'I believe that they did do some testing but not the actual manufacturing,' said Rosart unwillingly. 'The records aren't very explicit.'

'Anything else?' It was interesting, noted Sloan, how the information officer had immediately distanced himself from the unpalatable. The royal 'we' had suddenly become the impersonal 'they' when he spoke about the firm.

'A great deal else, naturally.'

'To do with dyes?'

'Mostly.'

'The Garamonds,' Sloan said. 'What did they do? Do you know?'

'Not exactly, Inspector, but I understand from such records as there are that to start with their work was to do with the staining of human cells.'

Sloan said that he couldn't quite see where that could have come into the war effort.

'I believe, Inspector – that is, as far as I can make out – the boffins at the War Office were interested in the development of a skin dye with which they could identify prisoners-of-war on a semi-permanent basis.'

'A tattoo that faded over time?' supplied Sloan cogently.

'Exactly. I have found records which indicate that checks were made to see that such an application did not contravene the Geneva Convention.'

'Hence the combination of a chemist and a bio-chemist?' said Sloan. Surely it was only the British who thought that war should be fought according to the Queensbury Rules?

Scrupulously.

Even if the other side played dirty.

'Very probably, Inspector. However, I understand that the project – it was codenamed Operation Tell-tale – came to nothing and it was abandoned after the works were bombed.'

'Chernwoods' Dyestuffs wanted her papers as of last week,' said Sloan flatly. 'You said so on Saturday when you rang the Grange . . .'

'Yes . . .'

'And from the state of the Grange at Great Primer it looks as if someone else wanted her papers pretty badly, too,' said Sloan, 'and not, unless I'm very much mistaken, just for old times' sake.'

'So it would seem.' A thin trickle of perspiration had appeared just below Gregory Rosart's hair-line.

'Therefore,' Sloan continued logically, 'it would also seem that Mrs Garamond's papers can't have been deposited with you here or even left behind at any time . . .'

'They haven't,' said Rosart quickly.

Too quickly.

That meant that Gregory Rosart had already checked. And had had a reason for checking.

'What is it, then,' said Detective Inspector Sloan, 'that you here at Chernwoods' wanted from Mrs Garamond's effects?' He addressed both men but Claude Miller made no move to answer him.

Gregory Rosart stumbled. 'I . . . that is, we . . . don't know.'

'But there is something . . .'

'Yes . . . no . . . that is, we think there might have been,' said the information officer.

'But you don't know what?' For some reason best known to himself, Detective Constable Crosby suddenly started to take an interest in the proceedings.

Rosart turned in the constable's direction. 'No, not exactly.'

'But,' said Sloan silkily, 'something happened that made you think that there might be . . . er . . . something?'

'I suppose you could put it like that.'

'And that Mrs Garamond's papers might be able to tell you what it was?'

This time it was chairman Claude Miller who fielded the question. 'Yes, Inspector.'

'Why did you wait until she was dead?' asked Sloan.

'We didn't.' Miller pointed ingenuously to Rosart. 'Greg here made several approaches by letter and in person.'

'Too right, I did,' said Rosart feelingly.

'And Mrs Garamond wouldn't see him. That's right, Greg, isn't it?' appealed Claude Miller.

The information officer nodded. 'For starters I couldn't get past the dragon at the gate.'

Sloan did a rapid search of his memory. 'Ellen? Her old maid?'

'More like a sentry on guard duty,' riposted Rosart.

'The letters?'

'Not answered. Any more than the telephone calls were responded to,' said Rosart. 'No joy in any direction.'

'I see.' Sloan settled himself more comfortably in his chair. 'And are you going to tell me what it was that suddenly provoked your interest?'

After a quick glance at his chairman, Rosart said: 'About six months ago we suddenly started to get a number of requests for information – which we turned down – about the work done here in the old days. They came from someone who described himself as a historian doing research for a thesis.'

'We had his story checked out, Inspector,' supplemented the chairman, 'and it didn't stand up.'

'I see.' Sloan maintained his leisurely posture. 'And then?'

'The next thing was an offer from a business history specialist willing to write us up for our hundred and fiftieth anniversary.'

'Which, I take it, would have involved giving the writer access to all your records?' asked Sloan.

'Exactly,' said Miller.

Sloan waited. 'Well?'

Claude Miller said, 'So Greg here started digging around for himself just in case and . . .'

'And?' prompted Sloan.

Rosart said slowly: 'There was nothing that I could put my finger on except what might have been a codename, Inspector. Nothing more than that . . .'

'A codename?'

'OZ.'

Detective Constable Crosby sat up. 'The Wonderful Wizard of?'

Rosart said, 'Your guess is as good as mine. But Operation something is more likely.'

'This codename,' said Sloan. 'Where did it crop up?'

'In an expenses claim for Hut Eleven towards the end of 1943. For an additional supply of microscope slides.'

'That all?' said Sloan. Not even an intolerable deal of sack to go with the half-pennyworth of bread? Sir John Falstaff would have done better than that.

'It was only because there seems to have been something of a legend attached to Hut Eleven that we looked at it twice . . .'

'The legend of Hut Eleven?' mused Sloan. Superintendent Leeyes wouldn't like that for sure. If there was any melodrama about the superintendent himself liked to be its 'onlie begetter'.

'I don't know much about it myself,' the information officer hastened on, 'just this rumour which still persists that they'd stumbled on something, but there was nothing in any records that we could find.'

'But surely, gentlemen,' said Sloan, who knew next to nothing about chemicals but a great deal about theft, 'any work done here by an employee remains the property of the company?'

'Indeed, yes, Inspector.' Miller was emphatic. 'We have a whole department here which deals with patents, copyright, intellectual property, and so forth.' He waved a long thin arm in the direction of the information officer. 'And one of Greg's jobs here is to – er – monitor beforehand' – *Censor*, translated Sloan; but not aloud – 'what we publish on – er – our findings' – *Discoveries*, thought Sloan to himself – 'that are – which might be – commercially sensitive.'

'And what, might I ask, was Hut Eleven?' asked Sloan,

who knew exactly what the chairman of Chernwoods' Dyestuffs meant by the words 'commercially sensitive'.

Valuable.

Rosart answered that one. 'In the war, Inspector, the people here at Chernwoods' worked in small huts out in the fields in case of air raids. There was a company rule that there were never to be more than ten workers in each hut at any one time.'

Detective Inspector Sloan nodded. Nowadays firms made much the same rule about those employees from any one department joining the same football pools' syndicate. The reasoning was the same in both instances: the employer didn't want to risk losing all the specialist workers in any one area of expertise at the same time.

'Would I be right,' Sloan said, 'in hazarding that Mr and Mrs Garamond worked in Hut Eleven?'

'You would.' Gregory Rosart gave a sigh of resignation. 'Both of them.'

'And who else?'

'Ah, Inspector, there we have had a little difficulty . . .' said Rosart. 'It was all so long ago, you see.'

'There are people we can't trace,' put in Claude Miller, 'although we'd like to.'

'Dead or alive?' Detective Constable Crosby made one of his rare interjections.

'Either,' said Claude Miller tersely.

'Both,' said Gregory Rosart in the same breath.

TWELVE

Shallow his grave and the dogs get him out

Amelia sat at the kitchen table for a long time after she had talked to the Bursar of Boleyn College trying to think of what she should do next.

She would have liked to go back to the Grange at Great Primer but the police had asked her not to do that yet. She had thought that if she just stood in the house she might pick up some feeling of what her great-aunt's death really meant. But there was little chance, anyway, she decided realistically, of her sensing any atmosphere at the Grange if the police were still going over it . . .

She would have liked to study much more carefully the old photograph of the wayside cross which James Puckle had handed over to her but Phoebe had taken that back with her to her medical consulting rooms where there was a really substantial magnifying glass that outdid any domestic one.

She would have liked to know who Kate was – she who had been left a candle – and to go over again the list of newspapers that Great-Aunt Octavia had asked to be notified of her death in order to see what she could glean from that but the details were still wtih Tod Morton and she didn't want to bother him again.

That left her with only the birth certificate.

The birth certificate at least, thought Amelia, was tangible and evidence that she hadn't dreamed the whole improbable affair. She took it up from the table and studied it once more. The birth certificate of an unknown woman about whom she knew nothing . . . well, not quite nothing. At least she knew the names her natural mother had bestowed on her – Erica Hester Goudy – even if they weren't the names used by her in after life.

And she knew, surely, that if she had been born in 1940 she must be middle-aged now. What she did not know, of course, was whether she was dead or alive. Looking for a nameless woman was going to be difficult: looking for an anonymous dead one would be pretty nearly impossible.

She continued to regard the piece of official paper in her hand. As she did so something that the History Man at her college had often quoted came unbidden into her mind.

'Documents,' he'd insisted time and time again to his students, 'don't speak to strangers . . .'

It was true, Amelia decided. This particular document was saying hardly anything at all to her. Perhaps she should try to remedy that. She wandered through the house into her father's study. At least she could learn something about 1940.

She looked at the shelves – there were bound to be books about the twentieth century there, to say nothing of books about war, since war and anthropology must surely be inseparable; or was that thought too cynical? Her father wasn't here to argue the point with her and so she applied herself instead to finding a book that would tell her what had been happening in England in 1940. That had been in what she always thought of as the last of the black and white wars. The Great War had been where the film was of men walking jerkily. In films of the Second World War men moved smoothly – but still in black and white.

There would be a scheme to her father's library shelves if only she could work it out. Her father had never minded her reading any of his books and had been willing to explain most – only balking once that she remembered. That had been when she had picked out when very young Sir James Frazer's *The Golden Bough*, taken by the title and thinking it a children's story.

His only request ever was that she put any book back from where she'd got it. He'd say, 'These are my tools, Amelia, and I need to be able to find them just like the mechanic in the garage does.'

Now she ran her fingers along the shelves, looking for some books to tell her about 1940 and, sure enough, she soon found a small row of them. She tried E. S. Turner's *The Phoney War* first as sound background; Margery Allingham's *The Oaken Heart* she put aside for a good read later. Evelyn Waugh's *Put Out More Flags* she left on the shelf. She was either too young or too old for the works of Evelyn Waugh – she didn't know which – and then she found Winston Churchill's history of the war. That would do to start with.

The section entitled 'The Twilight War: A Dark New Year' gave her somewhere to begin. The early months of 1940 seemed to have been devoted to sending British Army divisions to France: and, by the Germans, to preparing to attack Norway. By the middle of March Russia had crushed Finland and on the 18th of that month Hitler met Mussolini on the Brenner Pass.

And, it would seem, by then Octavia Harquil-Grasset had conceived a daughter.

Amelia went back to Winston Churchill's stirring narrative. He had become Prime Minister on 10th May 1940, offering nothing but 'blood, toil, tears, and sweat', the day when Hitler's armies had marched into the Low Countries. Something Amelia had never heard of called the British Expeditionary Force, flanked by Belgian and French divisions, was moving against the enemy forces when the front was broken.

She read on in the stillness of the library, strangely

stirred by the prose of war, her reading only stopped by her eye happening upon a word she did know – Dunkirk. Churchill had written of 'the deliverance of Dunkirk' in the last week of May and the first week of June.

By then, calculated Amelia, according to Phoebe, Octavia Harquil-Grasset must have known for certain, mice, frogs, and rabbits notwithstanding, that she was pregnant – and that there would be blood, toil, tears, and sweat ahead for her, too, never mind Great Britain.

Amelia turned back to Winston Churchill, seeking the history of another month in that year of peril.

December.

On 15th December 1940 Octavia Harquil-Grasset had given birth to a live female infant in a London already facing attack from the air. And given birth, too, apparently without benefit of clergy, so to speak. Her mind skipped back to the egregious Mr Fournier: did he know about Erica Hester Goudy's *sub rosa* birth? And was this why he was so reluctant to take her great-aunt's funeral service? Or had it been because he was a fundamentalist and her great-aunt a Darwinian biological scientist?

Answer – not unnaturally – coming there none, she went back to Churchill. There was nothing *sub rosa* about Churchill. He was, Amelia decided, a man you felt you knew where you were with. She sat on alone in the quiet study considering whether she had extracted all that she possibly could from the birth certificate.

There was just one more thing that she could do while she was among her father's books and that was to look up the meaning of the word 'mitosis' in the dictionary, since it was the study of this in sugar beet that had gained her great-aunt her essay prize at Boleyn.

Amelia said the definition aloud to herself when she found it but was really no wiser: 'the process of the division of the nucleus of a cell into minute threads'.

*

'Where do we stand then, Sloan?' There was every evidence that Superintendent Leeyes was about to leave his office.

'Difficult to say, sir,' said Sloan. The superintendent's wastepaper basket was on its side, which was a sure sign that his superior had devoted at least some of that afternoon to practising the ancient art of putting.

Leeyes grunted, one eye fixed on the clock. 'You'd better try all the same.'

'There's a firm in Luston called Harris and Marsh's Chemicals which is behaving as if it wants to take over Chernwoods' Dyestuffs, which fact may or may not be having any bearing on the business in hand.'

'And a death that the doctors can't make their minds up about . . .' chipped in Leeyes. 'Don't forget that.'

'It must happen sometimes . . .'

'Voltaire said that the practice of medicine was murderous and largely conjectural. Did you know that, Sloan?'

'No, sir,' said Sloan. Voltaire must have been a legacy from the superintendent's brief attendance at an Adult Education class on 'Famous French Writers'. The class had been notable at the police station for lasting only three sessions before the lecturer resigned, very hurt. Inspector Harpe from Traffic Division had been the winner of an informal sweepstake on the point within the station at the time.

'So . . .' said Leeyes.

'So we're on "hold" as far as Mrs Garamond's actual death is concerned, and are continuing to investigate the circumstances surrounding it.'

'Sloan,' said Leeyes dangerously, 'you're beginning to sound like a walking press release . . .'

'Sorry, sir . . .'

'Well, get on with it, man.'

'There's not a lot to tell, sir, at this stage. I am trying to establish whether Mrs Garamond's holding in her old firm was large enough to be significant in take-over terms.'

'And whether, if so, if she was killed to knock it into Tom Tiddler's Ground,' said the superintendent briskly, having no very high opinion of lawyers either.

'That, too, sir. I shall have to see James Puckle about the actual size of it. Miss Kennerley can't tell me; and I'm still awaiting a full report from Forensic on any useful traces left at the break-in at the Grange.'

'Anything else?' asked Leeyes.

'I think we're going to need to know a good deal more about Chernwoods' Dyestuffs, and the work the deceased and her late husband did there.'

'You've got a reason, I take it?'

'Mrs Garamond was very insistent that a notice of her death appeared in their staff magazine.' Sloan produced his notebook. 'I have been given a note of the people with whom she worked most closely in her early days there. That is to say, those who are believed to be still alive.'

'I think we are agreed, Sloan, that dead men tell no tales.'

'Yes, sir,' said Sloan, although in fact he was not at all sure that he did agree with the proposition. Who was it who had said, 'I look to Science for the cure of Crime'? True forensic scientists didn't require the living, surely, for all their observations . . .

'Well?'

'Mrs Garamond worked – er – especially closely during the war with nine other people – seven men and two women. Six of the ten have died over the years leaving three men and one woman still alive. They are called Nicholas Cochin, Catherine Camus, Martin Dido, and Albert Harris . . .'

'Any connection,' said Leeyes smartly, 'with Harris and Marsh's Chemicals Ltd. also of Luston?'

'Founder, and father of the present chairman,' said Sloan, 'but said to be mentally frail and now in a nursing home.'

'Check that out,' said Leeyes darkly. 'People sometimes get put away like that because it suits other people.'

'Yes, sir.' Sloan coughed. 'I shall in any case endeavour to follow up all Mrs Garamond's living colleagues as soon as I can . . .'

'Do that,' said Leeyes.

'Because it looks as if she tried very hard to make sure that someone – we don't know who – got to know about her death.'

'Then you'd better find out,' said the superintendent, reaching for his coat.

Detective Inspector Sloan, given this non-verbal *congé*, went back to his own office. There was a note waiting for him on his desk from Dyson, the police photographer, saying that he was attending to a serious case of hunger and thirst in the canteen. If D. I. Sloan cared to join him there in due course he might learn something to his advantage.

Sloan turned up at Dyson's table in the police canteen with a plateful of ham sandwiches and a mug of tea in his hands.

'I didn't realize how hungry I was,' remarked Sloan, 'until I saw food again.'

'I don't think they've heard of office hours in the Force, for all that they take on civilian employees,' said Dyson. 'I shan't tell you when I got home Saturday night, but if you saw a big woman cruising round the streets of Berebury with a frying pan at the ready it was my wife. She pretty nearly murdered me, I can tell you, as I was that late, and when I told her what I'd been doing, she started on at me all over again.'

'And what had you been doing?' asked Sloan between mouthfuls.

'Photographing a carpet.'

'Interesting?'

'Very.'

'Say on.'

'You know you told me that whoever had been in the Grange stirring things up had worn something over their shoes?'

'Yes.'

'That checked with what traces I found on the carpets – lovely carpets, by the way,' said Dyson, draining his mug.

'She was a rich woman,' said Detective Inspector Sloan. 'Go on.'

'Well, they'd made an impression on the carpet . . .'

'Naturally.'

'And so had the shoes that the two undertaker's men who came to collect the body wore and the woman, Shirley Whatsit, who spent the night there and found the old lady dead in the morning.'

'And those of the doctor who examined her?' said Sloan.

'Them, too. I photographed the lot,' said Dyson. 'This new camera I've got did them a real treat. I've told you about my new camera, haven't I?'

'Several times,' said Sloan.

'Well, I've developed the films today and I must say they've come up a real treat, too.'

'What did you find?'

Dyson leaned forward and said: 'What would you say, Inspector, if I was to tell you that I've got as clear a print as any court would want of that carer woman's shoe over as clear a print as any court would want of one of Mr Unknown's fudged ones?'

'I should say, Dyson,' said Sloan giving the photographer an appraising look, 'that it's high time you had a second mug of tea and that it will give me very great pleasure to get it for you.'

THIRTEEN

Bury him softly – white wool around him

There was at least one member of the City of London's police force whose uniform was a black suit with pinstripe trousers, and who was armed not with the regulation wooden truncheon but with a tightly rolled black umbrella.

His speciality was white-collar crime and his beat the environs of the Stock Exchange. To him a balance sheet was as clear a map as the back of his hand, traded options part of his daily routine. He declared himself over the phone only too happy to discuss any little local financial difficulty with Detective Inspector C.D. Sloan of the Calleshire Force and said he had the papers before him, thank you.

'Is there any clue in Chernwoods' Dyestuffs' balance sheet and annual accounts as to why Harris and Marsh's Chemicals should want to take them over?' asked Sloan, going straight to the point.

'Not that I can see, old chap.' Some of the vernacular of business seemed to have rubbed off on the specialist because he said: 'I've cast the optic over them and I should say that Chernwoods' Dyestuffs' trading position is pretty average for that sector. Bit below, if anything, actually.'

'But . . .'

'Exactly, Inspector, *but* someone's been buying into them lately, all right. And quite heavily, too, in spite of their having had the odd hiccup in their last trading year.'

'Hiccup?' said Sloan cautiously. Detection could be hindered by hiccups. Or helped.

'They seem to have their problems,' said the voice, 'such as a fire in their packing department and a big claim for breach of intellectual property rights – that's pinching somebody else's ideas to you and me – and the odd boardroom row.'

'They're not exactly a jewel in the chemical research crown, then?' said Sloan.

'Keeping trading from sheer force of habit, I should say. Been doing it for long enough. My sources tell me that Chernwoods' present chairman is a chip off the old blockhead his father was. Weak, too.'

'He's the third generation,' said Sloan.

'Mind you,' said the specialist, 'all these chemical companies depend on their latest compound doing better than the new compound invented by the fellow down the road. Or anywhere else in the world, in fact.'

'I see.' Sloan would have to submerge the rest of the world without trace when reporting to Superintendent Leeyes. The superintendent's cosmography went no further than the county boundary of Calleshire. So far no one had thought fit to tell him that it had been William the Conqueror who had determined English county boundaries . . .

'And,' continued the City man, 'with this sort of company there's always the difficulty of having very big money tied up in research for years at a time. Until a breakthrough pays for the next decade.'

'Or doesn't?' said Sloan.

'True. Then they'd start to welcome predators. Preferably with long purses for severance pay-outs to the board and senior staff . . .'

'Or a promise to keep them on?'

'Not if they've got any sense,' said the voice in London

frankly. 'If the old guard was any good in the first place they'd have been taken over themselves by the big boys long ago.'

'We're talking about small fry, then?' said Sloan, unsurprised. Nature was, it seemed, as red in tooth and claw in the Square Mile as it was everywhere else.

'Relatively speaking. I dare say both companies are pretty big fish in your neck of the woods . . .'

'It's a small pond,' conceded Sloan, who could mix a metaphor as well as the next man.

'The other thing that would have happened if Chernwoods' Dyestuffs was worth picking up,' said the money-man at the other end of the line, 'is that they would have been doing some natty taking-over on their own account, and there's no sign of that having happened that I can find in either their figures or annual reports.'

'So,' said Sloan, anxious to get one thing clear, 'if this Chernwoods' outfit had some really marketable ideas in the pipeline someone would have snapped them up long ago unless they had been very secretive?'

'Exactly. The big boys are always on the look-out for other people's discoveries, and they're not too fussy about how they get hold of 'em,' said the voice. 'Since we're talking about fish you can think of them as pike.'

'Pike?' That parallel would be very difficult to convey to the superintendent.

'Big, greedy, omnivorous, and lurking in muddy waters for whatever it can sink its teeth into,' said the man in London. 'And as tough as old boots.'

'I get you,' said Sloan. Suddenly, being a policeman combating ordinary crime out in the sticks began to seem more attractive. 'Now, can you also tell me, please, if there is anything about Harris and Marsh's Chemicals that might make them ripe for carrying out a take-over of Chernwoods' Dyestuffs?'

'No. Neither outfit seems to have come up with anything really worthwhile for quite a time. That's the really interesting thing about the whole situation. It doesn't make commercial sense.'

Detective Inspector Sloan made a note: all good policemen were by nature connoisseurs of the unusual, not to say the improbable.

'In my opinion,' continued the financial expert, 'Harris and Marsh would just be adding to their existing burdens by taking over Chernwoods' Dyestuffs at this point in their mutual histories.'

'I see.' Something out of line should be meat and drink to a detective.

'In the first place Harris and Marsh's are very seriously under-funded by today's standards in that field,' said the voice calmly. 'And if Harris and Marsh's Chemicals are even contemplating offering one of their shares for two of Chernwoods' Ordinary or something fancy like that, then all I can say is that Chernwoods' board would want its head looking at as well.'

'Perhaps,' suggested Sloan a mite diffidently, 'they're simply going to buy into Chernwoods' Dyestuffs?'

'I don't know what with,' said the City man with spirit. 'There's not much in the way of cash reserves in these figures. And if they're going to borrow to do it then I wouldn't like to be their bankers.'

'So . . .' said Sloan.

'So either they don't know what they're doing,' said the voice down the line, 'and you can take it from me that happens more often than it should, or they're after something that Chernwoods' doesn't know it's got – let alone you and me and Joe Public – or Chernwoods' does know and isn't telling, which is only nearly legal, or . . .'

'Or?'

'Some fool has set his sights on getting control to satisfy his life's ambition – that happens at all levels with people who should know better. No, if they were to ask my advice . . .'

'Yes?' It sounded to Sloan very much a case of 'eat or be

eaten' in that jungle but he was always willing to learn.

'I'd say a merger would be the only possible course of action that would stand up commercially in the market, plus promoting or sacking their dissident chief chemist.'

'The word here,' ventured Sloan carefully, wishing he'd played the game of Monopoly with more attention, 'is that there's a possibility of a management buy-out at Chernwoods' Dyestuffs rather than be taken over by Harris and Marsh's Chemicals.'

'We heard that, too, and so I've had a word with one of my contacts about that, and my information,' said the City man cagily, 'is that that's being led by their aforementioned chief chemist, name of Joe Keen.'

Sloan made another note.

'I hear he's got a chip on his shoulder because they won't give him a seat on the board. That,' he added wisely, 'is when a lot of people tend to get upset.'

'How would a management buy-out work out with Chernwoods'?' asked Sloan. He'd like to see one of those tried down at the police station in 'F' Division, not that he really thought they'd ever get rid of Superintendent Leeyes that way.

'Well, they do say that there's one fool born every minute,' said the man in the City, sounding relaxed. 'You can't hope to save 'em from themselves, you know.'

'No . . .' That was a lesson learned early on in the Force.

'If I were you, Inspector,' he advised at a comfortable distance, 'I should keep your breath to cool your porridge and let 'em get on with it.'

'Ye–es.' It was all very well for the expert to think like that.

'Chernwoods' Dyestuffs sounds an unlucky firm to me and the stock market's pretty nearly as superstitious as Napoleon – it never likes unlucky generals.'

*

102

'You mean now, sir? As in like this minute?'

'Now, Crosby, as in now.' Detective Inspector Sloan consulted a piece of paper. 'The nursing home is on the road between Larking and Luston and is big enough not to be missed.'

'All I'm missing,' said Detective Constable Crosby plaintively, 'is food.'

'Old men in nursing homes who are said to be out of their minds can die as suddenly as old ladies who are said to have bad hearts,' said Sloan incisively. 'There's no time like the present in police work, Crosby. You should remember that.'

'Yes, sir.' The constable's rebellious tone was muted to a nicety. 'So it's important, then, is it, sir?'

'Either the good lady you interviewed didn't turn up at the Grange on Thursday night,' replied Sloan obliquely, 'and just went in first thing in the morning instead and found Mrs Garamond dead, or . . .'

'Or what, sir?'

'Or,' said Sloan ineluctably, 'whoever went in to search for something had also been in the deceased's bedroom during the night and there are photographs of footprints on other footprints to prove it.'

'Every picture tells a story,' observed the constable, putting his own foot down.

'And,' continued Detective Inspector Sloan, 'if they went into the deceased's bedroom in the night with a view to accelerating her death, Crosby, we have a case of murder on our hands.'

They did indeed find the nursing home without difficulty. It had begun life as a fine Victorian gentleman's residence and was now the last home of a number of members of that unfortunate group of patients known as psychogeriatric.

Mr Albert Harris was presently in a back bedroom no doubt once occupied by a poorly paid 'tween maid. She

103

would have been rich indeed in comparison with its current occupant. His bedclothes were in considerable disarray, and his night attire only covered unselected parts of his anatomy. He was all too obviously there in body but equally certainly absent in mind; and he could have played the latter days of King Lear on stage without change of costume or rehearsal.

'I'm a detective engaged on an investigation,' said Sloan slowly and clearly.

'Good,' said the old gentleman promptly. 'Someone's stolen my teeth.'

'He's broken three sets,' said the matron at his elbow. 'He throws them at the nurses.'

'I want to talk to you about Mrs Octavia Garamond,' said Sloan.

At the mention of that name a flicker of recognition passed over the old man's face and Albert Harris, senior, clamped his toothless jaws shut.

Sloan turned aside and said to the matron in a low voice that he wanted to tell Mr Harris, *père*, about the death of an old colleague but didn't want to upset him.

'You won't upset him, Inspector, I promise you,' she said wearily. 'It's the nurses who get upset here, not the patients.'

Detective Inspector Sloan said: 'Mr Harris, do you remember Hut Eleven?'

'You're not my son,' piped Mr Harris.

'No, I'm not your son.'

'There was a war on,' said the old chap. 'Want my teeth, Nurse . . .'

'There was a war on,' agreed Sloan. 'What was Octavia Garamond doing in Hut Eleven at Chernwoods'?'

'Rikki-Tikki-Tavi,' croaked the man in the bed. 'Rikki-Tikki-Tavi.'

'I'm sorry, Inspector,' apologized the matron, 'it's not one of his better days.'

' "Good, better, best," ' chanted Harris, in high cracked tones, ' "never let it rest, until the good is better and the better best." '

'What was good about Hut Eleven?' asked Sloan.

The edentulous face of Albert Harris assumed a remarkably cunning expression. 'Mustn't talk about Hut Eleven,' he said. 'Mustn't ever talk about Hut Eleven to anyone. Not ever.'

'You can talk to me,' said Detective Inspector Sloan persuasively. 'Tell me what Rikki-Tikki-Tavi did.'

The old man grabbed his crumpled sheet and pulled it over his head.

'Was it anything to do with Operation Tell-tale?' Sloan asked.

The sheet was flung back and Albert Harris said: 'Mustn't tell tales.'

'No,' agreed Sloan pacifically, 'you mustn't. Tell me about OZ instead.'

Albert Harris suddenly burst into song. In the childish treble of the sixth age of man he burst into 'The Wonderful Wizard of Oz'.

'Who was the wonderful Wizard of Oz?' asked Sloan.

'Rikki-Tikki-Tavi, or course,' responded the old man, suddenly looking quite rational. 'Everyone knows that.' He stared at Sloan's face. 'I don't know you. Who are you, anyway?'

'Someone who wants to know all about Hut Eleven and the others. Like Nicholas Cochin . . .'

'Fred's dead,' remarked the old man inconsequentially. 'Poor Fred.'

'Not Fred, Mr Harris. Nicholas Cochin . . .'

'He didn't know.'

'Know what?'

Harris's face clouded. 'Don't know anything.'

'Catherine Camus?'

'No flies on Kate . . .' The rationality came back

momentarily and then the jaw clamped shut again. 'Who are you?'

'And Martin Didot?'

'You're not Martin Didot,' said Albert Harris peering at him.

'No, I'm not Martin Didot, but I want to know about him.'

'He was only the boy.' Albert Harris put out a hand and clutched Sloan's arm with quite surprising strength for such a spindleshanks. 'Where's Fred?'

Getting no answer to this he began to rock himself backwards and forwards in the bed, chanting: 'Poor Fred, Fred's dead . . .'

'Sometimes,' the matron said as she shepherded the two policemen out, 'he's quite good and sometimes he's quite demented. You can never tell.'

If this was one of Albert Harris's better days, Sloan didn't like to think what his bad ones were like.

FOURTEEN

Kiss his poor feathers – first kiss and last

Amelia sat on in her father's study for a long time, her mind a gallimaufry of all that she had been told and had read that day. Only last week – it seemed aeons ago now – only this time last week she and Mary-Louise had walked up the hill to the *bastide* village of Domme and photographed the picturebook landscape of the Dordogne river valley below.

Mary-Louise had quoted Goethe's remark about no view being worth looking at for more than fifteen minutes and Amelia had contested this: and then conceded defeat after ten long minutes by succumbing instead to the even more tempting prospect of a *chocolat Liègois*.

Her reverie in the study was brought to an end by the telephone bell.

'It's Dr Phoebe's secretary,' said a girl's voice. 'She's asked me to ring you to say she'll be very late back tonight and not to wait supper for her.'

'Thank you for letting me know,' said Amelia automatically.

'She said to tell you that she's got to go over to a clinical meeting at the Calleford Infirmary this evening but she said I should say that she's had a look at your photograph under the magnifier . . .'

'Yes?'

'She thinks she can make out what might be a motto at the top . . .'

Amelia pulled a piece of paper towards her. 'Let me find a pen . . . yes, all right, go ahead.'

'She is almost sure it says *"Nec temere"* . . .'

'Latin?'

'I couldn't say, I'm sure,' said the secretary.

'Sorry. I didn't mean to interrupt you . . .'

'She thinks,' said the secretary, spelling it out, 'that it says *"Nec temere, nec timide"*.'

'Nothing else?' said Amelia urgently.

'Not that Dr Phoebe could see with the magnifier here . . .'

Amelia put the telephone down and then glanced quickly at her watch. She would ring Montpazier: the others would be bound to be back by now from wherever they had been for the day and be turning their minds to dinner.

Getting through was easy, getting to the point of her call not so. Mary-Louise was full of questions and sympathy. 'We're fine, Milly, dear, but what about you?'

'I'll tell you all about it later,' she promised. 'Mary-Louise, tell me what *"Nec temere, nec timide"* means . . .'

'Neither rashly, nor fearfully,' said the language specialist immediately. 'Listen, Milly, you really must come back here one day. We've had a marvellous outing today to an old castle called Bonaguil, and now we're sitting on the *terrasse* with a kir before we eat . . .'

It was another world.

And about as remote as the Moon, Amelia decided, glancing at the clock before going for her jacket and slipping out quickly into the town.

'Berebury Hospital switchboard here,' said a girl's voice. 'Could Detective Inspector Sloan take a call from Dr Dabbe?'

'He could,' said Sloan warmly. 'Sloan speaking . . .'

'Ah, Sloan, I've just been talking to an old friend,' said the pathologist.

'Have you?' said Sloan more warily. It was difficult to imagine anyone who was as cold-blooded as Dr Dabbe having family, let alone friends.

'Met him the first day we did anatomy,' reminisced the pathologist. 'Shared a leg with him donkey's years ago at our first human dissection.'

'Did you?' said Sloan discouragingly.

'Been friends ever since,' said Dabbe enthusiastically. 'Funny how often you become friends with the chap you share a limb with.'

'Very,' responded Sloan, who felt a blinder blind date would be impossible to envisage. And why a dead leg should lead to bosom friendship, he couldn't begin to think. It must have done, though, because the pathologist went on: 'Agate did very well for himself afterwards – went in for toxicology, got a professorship, writes textbooks and all that sort of thing . . .'

'Good,' said Sloan vaguely.

'He was first-rate even as a student – I've never forgotten the way he explored that first knee . . .'

'Haven't you?' said Sloan restrainedly.

'Well, I sent him a bit of that old lady's liver for an opinion – thought that he'd be interested and like to have it anyway . . .'

'And?' said Sloan. The pathologist seemed to have reduced the whole business of autopsy and police investigation in one easy step to the level of two schoolboys swapping comics.

'He wants to see a lung section,' said Dabbe happily. 'He says that the presence of one of the halogenated hydrocarbons can't be ruled out. He thinks he might just be able to isolate one of the agents there.'

'Does he?' said Sloan, who didn't like being blinded by science. 'And what are they?' He also had a rooted objection to being made to seem foolish by mispronouncing words he didn't know.

'Good question,' said the pathologist. 'They're a big

group of chemical nasties used mostly as industrial cleaning agents and agricultural growth accelerators.'

'I see.' Sloan turned a page in his notebook over. 'Industrial, did you say?'

'My old pal Agate – we called him Stony, of course – says he thinks that there might have been some substance containing one of these halogenated carbons administered to the deceased . . .'

'Does he?' said Sloan, the words 'think' and 'might' being a trifle too circumspect for a detective inspector – any detective inspector.

'In Agate's opinion something has left traces in the liver and kidneys sections which could well be consistent with ethylene poisoning.'

'I see,' said Sloan. Agate, whoever he was, had learned professional caution over the years. Opinions were something that anyone could hold: and did.

'The halogenated hydrocarbons are a very volatile group,' said the pathologist.

'But Dr Aldus said she'd died from heart failure,' pointed out Sloan. The superintendent could be very volatile, too: especially when presented with conflicting medical statements.

'And so she did,' said the pathologist stoutly. 'The mode of death would have been respiratory and circulatory failure – which is precisely what Dr Aldus expected her to die from.'

'But . . .'

'It is the cause of death that we are discussing now, Sloan, not the mode. That's something quite different.'

'So what you are saying, doctor,' Detective Inspector Sloan was not prepared to play hair-splitting games with specialists, 'is that Mrs Garamond's death could have been as a result of her having inhaled something?'

'A noxious substance,' said Dr Dabbe.

'Poison gas, you mean?'

'Let us say rather that it might have been a gas that was poisonous,' qualified the doctor.

'I see,' said Sloan. Any minute now they would be arguing how many angels could dance on the head of a pin.

'There were those marks still on her face . . .' said Dabbe.

'I'll have that oxygen cylinder checked out straight away,' said Sloan, making a note. 'Of course, doctor, if it was one of these halogen things you were talking about . . .'

'Halogenated hydrocarbons,' supplied the doctor obligingly.

'Then that could mean we would be dealing with somebody who knew what they were doing chemically.'

'Well,' conceded Dr Dabbe, 'you wouldn't exactly pick 'em up in a child's home chemistry set.'

'I was beginning to think that might be the case,' said the detective inspector, pulling his notebook towards him and writing Chernwoods' Dyestuffs and Harris and Marsh's Chemicals at the head of the next page.

'What my friend would like to know,' continued Dabbe, 'and me, too, of course, Sloan, naturally – is whether there is anyone whom you might just be happening to be keeping an eye on who might know their chemical onions so to say.'

'Yes,' said Sloan unenthusiastically.

'Ah . . . good man. Agate said it might help a lot if we know what any suspects could get hold of easily.'

'A little matter of the work forces of two firms of manufacturing chemists,' Sloan said, adding meaningfully, 'plus everyone who has ever worked for the said firms. And, doctor, that's only for starters . . .'

He had already added the name of Dr John Aldus to his list.

*

111

''Ullo, 'ullo,' said Tod Morton when Crosby walked in to the undertaker's yard back in Nethergate Street, in Berebury. 'What's all this here then?'

'Pinching my lines, if nothing else,' declared the detective constable. 'I could book you for that, Tod Morton, but I won't.'

The undertaker held up his hands in mock surrender and said: 'All right, all right. I shan't say "Let's be having you . . ." '

'Just as well,' growled Crosby.

'Because I'll get you in the end,' said Tod, winking. 'I get everybody in the end, you know.'

'I'm pursuing police enquiries, that's what I'm doing, Tod Morton, and I'd be obliged for your assistance.'

'Pursue away,' invited Tod amiably.

'We're just checking on the particulars of that girl, name of Baskerville, who was seen at the Grange at Great Primer by the rector last Friday afternoon.'

'Again?'

'Well, we haven't found her yet,' said Crosby naïvely, 'and we'd rather like to talk to her.'

'I'll bet.'

'There's no call for you to take that line with me, Tod Morton,' said Crosby, stung. 'She may have no connection at all with our enquiries.'

'What enquiries?' said Tod blandly.

'Never you mind,' retorted Crosby importantly. 'What I want to know is can you add anything to what you told us Saturday?'

Tod screwed up his face in recollection. 'No, 'fraid not.'

'Age?'

''Bout twenty-five, give or take a year or two.'

'Height?' asked Crosby, taking out his notebook. 'What would you say?'

'Five foot six inches.'

'Sure?'

The undertaker grinned. 'Height's the one thing I'm always sure about.'

'Oh?'

'Dead sure. Get it?'

'No.'

'Oh, well, you can take it from me that the girl was five six.'

'How do you kn—'

'And,' said Tod, eyeing the young detective constable appraisingly, 'you're five foot eleven and a half, aren't you?'

Crosby's head came up with a jerk. 'I'm regulation police height . . .'

'In your stockinged feet,' added Tod.

'Well, I'll be blowed . . .'

'Practice makes perfect,' said Tod modestly, adding, 'I could do you a coffin straight off the shelf, too, if you wanted one, but I'll give you a cup of tea instead. Come along indoors with me.' He led the way towards the building. Over his shoulder he said: 'Have you heard about the seven-foot man in Calleford that they can't bury?'

'No,' said Crosby. 'Why can't they bury him, then?'

'Because he's not dead.'

Detective Inspector Sloan hunched his shoulders forward in the passenger seat of the police car – always a sign that he was thinking hard – as Crosby slipped the vehicle through the late afternoon town traffic and headed for Great Primer.

'Dr Aldus is meeting us out there, Crosby,' Sloan said.

'Why he?' responded Crosby demotically.

'Inspector Harpe tells me he's heard that the good doctor could do with his legacy.'

'Wine, women, or song?' asked the detective constable.

113

'None of those,' said Sloan. 'We get the doctors who drink, remember, the General Medical Council gets those that go in for women, and there can't be a lot of song in a place like Great Primer, can there?'

'Gee-gees, then?' said Crosby. 'Slow horses instead of fast ladies?'

'That's what I'm told,' said Sloan.

'It's not a crime.'

'Much more expensive though.' He looked at his watch. 'I'd like us to be there first.'

He needn't have worried – and he knew he needn't have worried – about that. Whilst Crosby took the little country lanes as fast as he dared Sloan gave his mind to what he now knew to be a case of murder. Murder cleverly executed by some person or persons unknown using unusual expertise, which, had the victim not been on the alert, would have stood a very good chance of going undetected.

'We'd just like to run over one or two points again in connection with Mrs Octavia Garamond's murder,' Sloan said to Dr Aldus without preamble, 'with you here on the spot.'

He'd had the general practitioner summoned out to the Grange at Great Primer for several reasons, not the least of which was that in his own consulting room it was the doctor who was behind the desk. All three were now standing in the deceased's bedroom.

'Murder?' Aldus certainly looked startled enough. 'How was she murdered?'

'Now, I was rather hoping that you'd be able to help us over that, Doctor.'

'Me?' The general practitioner looked alarmed, the more especially perhaps because Detective Constable Crosby had his notebook very much at the ready.

'You saw her after she'd died,' said Sloan, suddenly a model of sweet reason. 'And you examined her body. At least,' he added, 'you said you had done.'

Aldus nodded vigorously. 'Certainly, I did. And, as I told you, I found nothing inconsistent with death from congestive heart failure.'

'The forensic specialists have,' said Sloan.

Aldus stared. 'I can assure you that there was no visible evidence of there having been anything at all – er – untoward about the death when I last saw my patient.'

'Maybe there wasn't any evidence to be seen,' posited Sloan.

'Or,' insisted John Aldus, ruffled, 'any single indication of foul play in the bedroom when I was sent for that I could see.'

'So you said, doctor, so you said.' For a wonder, thought Sloan, Crosby wasn't saying anything at all. It wasn't like him.

'I meant it.' Aldus looked across at the two policemen. 'Are you going to tell me how this murder was accomplished?'

'Probably while she was asleep,' said Sloan elliptically. 'Mrs Garamond was on sleeping tablets, wasn't she?'

'Yes.'

'A small dose or a big one?'

'The right dose of any medication, Inspector, is enough for it to do what you want it to do and not to do what you don't.'

'So?' Sloan dismissed this offering of medical philosophy with a wave of the hand without drawing any parallels with the good night's sleep apparently enjoyed at the Grange that night by Mrs Shirley Doves.

'So,' the doctor came back promptly, 'Mrs Garamond was on the right amount of a narcotic preparation to ensure her a good night's sleep without depressing her already compromised respiratory function.'

Sloan pointed to the double bed. 'Tell me, doctor, which side of the bed did the old lady sleep on?'

'This side,' said Aldus unhesitatingly. 'The one nearer the door.'

'You're sure?'

'Quite sure because I'm right-handed and therefore I examined her from this side.'

'Then why was her bed-light on the far side of the bed-head?' Sloan had remembered what it was that had teased his mind on his first visit here. 'She couldn't have reached the switch from this side of the bed.'

'I don't know. It wasn't usually there.'

'The oxygen cylinder was . . . where?'

'Where it is now – the further side. As you can see the tubing was long enough for the mask to reach the patient on this side of the bed.'

Sloan had already studied the mask which might or might not have left the ring-mark that the pathologist had noted on Mrs Garamond's face.

'Where was her bell?'

Dr Aldus frowned. 'I didn't notice. It was usually pinned to the top of her sheet.'

Sloan felt a sudden unprofessional wave of pity for a helpless old lady, dying alone, beyond aid and in the dark, help – the comfort of light, even – deliberately placed out of her reach. For her own sake he hoped that she had died unaware of her murderer and for the sake of justice he intended to arraign that same person.

It was a way of thinking that made the policeman out of the man.

FIFTEEN

Tell his poor widow kind friends have found him.

Gregory Rosart received his summons to the chairman's room just before the end of the afternoon. Joe Keen was already there, white-coated and outwardly impassive.

'Ah, there you are, Greg,' said Claude Miller fussily. 'Come in. We want your advice about a press release.'

Rosart looked swiftly from Claude Miller to Joe Keen and back again. 'A press release about what? We haven't made a breakthrough, have we?'

'Exactly,' said Keen. 'Just what I wanted to know, too.' He stared insultingly at a point somewhere over Claude Miller's shoulder. 'And, no, we haven't made a breakthrough.'

'I've just been on to our brokers again,' announced the chairman of Chernwoods', 'and they say Harris and Marsh have stopped buying all of a sudden.'

'Don't blame them,' said Joe Keen morosely. 'More fool them, I say, that they started to do it in the first place.' He exchanged another quick glance with Rosart. 'If they want to stop sending good money after bad now, then let 'em, but it's not news by a long chalk.'

The chairman of Chernwoods' winced but his chief chemist hadn't finished. 'I don't see how anyone can make the press interested in an attempt at a take-over . . .'

'But, Joe, if we were to tie it in with a product announcement . . .'

'Even though,' said Keen, 'I should say it's still going to turn into a hostile bid any minute now.'

Claude Miller opened his mouth to speak but Keen was unstoppable.

'Sorry to do you out of one of your famous photo-opportunities, Greg,' Keen said with patent insincerity, 'but if ever there was a time for a low profile, it's now.'

'I should have thought,' offered Greg Rosart carefully, 'that at this moment the fewer people who knew about what was going on between us the better.'

'So should I,' said Joe Keen at once.

'Honestly, Claude,' said the press officer before Miller could say anything, 'what Harris and Marsh are trying to—'

'Have been trying to do,' interposed Claude Miller. 'I tell you they've stopped.'

'Whatever,' said Rosart. 'It's not news either way. Take it from me, two lines at the bottom of the column in the financial papers is about all that Chernwoods' would get these days. And it wouldn't do us any good, Mr Miller, either.'

'We could tell them,' persisted Claude Miller, 'that the board of Chernwoods' is going to fight Harris and Marsh to the last ditch . . .' Miller was like many indecisive people in that when he did make up his mind to take action he did so obstinately and irrationally.

The silence of his two employees was as eloquent as any argument.

Eventually Greg Rosart said gently, 'I do think, Mr Miller, that we ought to go slowly on this. We could easily overdo the publicity side if we aren't careful . . .'

'What you really mean, Greg,' interrupted Joe Keen harshly, 'is that Chernwoods' has been in the papers quite enough already this year.'

Claude Miller opened his mouth to speak but couldn't get a word in edgeways.

'First of all,' enumerated Keen, 'we have a fire that can't be accounted for, then a prosecution by the Health

118

and Safety people for which we get a whopping fine and all the unfavourable publicity in the world' – he started to get to his feet as he spoke – 'and if that wasn't enough we have a successful claim against us for wrongful dismissal which shook the work force to its wattles.' He began to make for the door. 'No, thank you, Claude, if you're talking about last ditches, I vote that we keep our heads below the parapet from now on.'

Miller flushed and retorted angrily: 'You'll be glad enough, Joe, to have publicity when – if, that is – you ever come up with the compound that's going to make all our fortunes.'

'Then I'll arrange it myself,' snapped Keen, half-way through the door. 'Glad to.'

Amelia glanced at her watch as she hurried along through Berebury's streets to a shop opposite the market-place. She wanted to catch it before closing time. In the event she needn't have worried. Mr Henryson was still there, surrounded as always by piles of books, badges, old uniforms, and other relics of the battlefield, loosely called militaria.

She squeezed inside the door between a giant shell-case, which now did duty as an umbrella stand, and a rack of steel helmets from every war and country and period imaginable. The shop door of Undertones of War still had a bell that jangled as the customer went in and Mr Henryson looked up with the mild uninterest of the secondhand bookseller as Amelia entered. He had been deep in a book and certainly wouldn't have noticed her or anyone else but for the bell.

He nodded, keeping a finger at his place in the book. 'Want any help?'

'Please,' said Amelia. 'I'm not really sure myself what I'm looking for.'

'Ah,' said Mr Henryson gently.

119

'But I thought that you might be able to tell me.'

'I may,' he said, a soldier manqué, a fireside fusilier who had never been to war himself but who had made a long and diligent study of the god Mars and his descendants.

'I think I want a book about regimental mottos,' she said, 'but I don't know for sure. It's what you might call rather a long shot.' Now that she came to think of it, that expression had probably begun life as a military term.

'Tell me . . .' said Mr Henryson with mild interest.

'I want to know if "*Nec Temere, Nec Timide*" is a regimental motto.'

Mr Henryson stroked his chin in thought for a moment. 'Fortescue would know,' he said, 'Sir John is always very good. I haven't got a Swinson but we could see if F. Tytler Fraser . . .'

'Where would I find them?' she asked anxiously. 'It's rather important . . .'

'On the shelves over here, my dear.' Mr Henryson led the way towards the back of the shop. Stepping aside to avoid a stack of second-hand armour, Amelia followed him, negotiating her way round some Sam Brownes and what appeared to be inert limpet mines.

'This is even better,' he said reaching for a dust-covered volume. 'I think you'll find them all in here somewhere, if you don't mind doing a bit of research.'

'No, I don't mind,' she said eagerly. 'I've got to find it.'

'It'll take time,' he warned her. 'Especially if, like me, you tend to get carried away.' He smiled absently. 'I was just crossing the Somme when you came in.'

Amelia searched her memory. '1916?'

He shook his head. '1346. Crécy. I just can't see how our army got across it where we did. It would have been far too wide there and then for our people . . .'

'When are you due to close?' she asked him rather too directly.

'About half an hour ago,' he said, sounding genuinely apologetic. 'My wife doesn't like it if I'm too late because of keeping the supper hot. I have been known to forget supper altogether if I'm enthralled. Battlefields can be enthralling, you know. It's like dice and gambling. So much hangs on so little – the outcome, I mean.'

Amelia eyed the book he had found for her. It wasn't a very thick one and Phoebe wasn't going to be home until late. She said: 'If I was to go and have some supper in the White Hart . . .'

'I'm afraid Richard II was no soldier,' said the book-seller, 'white hart or not, but Edward III' – his eye gleamed – 'now he was different . . .'

'In the White Hart,' said Amelia, ignoring this tempting diversion, 'over the other side of the market, and slip this back through your letter-box when I've done with it, would that be all right?'

The book, propped up on the inn table, all about regiments, might not have been large but it was certainly densely printed. Amelia had both eaten and then had her coffee in the lounge before she was half-way through. She ordered more coffee and reapplied herself to studying the crests and badges of all the regiments, her eye inevitably straying to their battle honours too.

She was almost through the book – and very nearly asleep, too – when she came across the crest of the Fearnshires, the words *Nec temere, nec timide* suddenly staring out of the page at her. The Fearnshires, were, it seemed, a Highland Regiment of ancient origin, having their beginnings as 'men-at-arms' to the chief of their clan and only regularized and brought into line as members of the British Army after 1745 and the Battle of Culloden Moor ('otherwise known', ran the text, as impartially as it could, 'as Drumossie').

Amelia spotted a writing table in the corner of the inn's lounge and went across to pen Mr Henryson a note of thanks, adding a postscript asking him if he had by any chance got a copy of the regimental history of the Fearnshires for sale in his shop. She tucked this missive into the book, pushed both through the letter-box of Undertones of War, and set off through the streets of Berebury for home, quite surprised to find how late it now was.

Someone else late home that evening was Detective Inspector C.D. Sloan: so late that even Madame Caroline Testout did not get her customary evening visit, whilst 'the son who should have lisped his sire's return' had been long in bed and asleep.

At some time in every policeman's life he himself has to decide how much of his work he could or should talk to his wife about. The ideal was somewhere between the 'nothing' advised by those who trained him and the 'everything' advocated by those whose professional concern was with marriages lasting. How soon after marriage that a man took the decision was important, too . . .

The old sergeant who had taught him a lot in his early days in the Force had always counselled him along the lines of the old advertisement for shaving soap – 'not too little, not too much, but just right', adding: 'But whatever you do, lad, never tell her when to expect you home. The night you're late back she'll have you dead and buried within the hour and you'll never hear the last of it.'

In the event Sloan had done what most men did. He brought home palatable titbits from the day's work and hid the dreariness and the danger under the cloak of the pedestrian and routine.

Tonight was slightly different. Pushing his now empty plate to one side, he asked his wife, Margaret, how many words she knew beginning with the letter 'Z'.

'Zigzag,' said Margaret, frowning. 'Zircon . . .'

'Zebra . . .' said the policeman.

'Zero,' said his wife.

Sloan capped that with: 'Zenith . . . oh, and Zenana.' His grandmother had always been a great supporter of Zenana missions.

'Zeus,' contributed Margaret Sloan, 'or aren't real names allowed?'

'We don't know. We think the "O" stands for "Operation" but the "Z" could be for anything.'

'Zeppelin?'

'Could be. All this "OZ" stuff was going on in the last war. Then there's always Zion,' added Sloan, dutiful son of a church-going mother.

'Isn't there a musical instrument . . .'

'Zither,' said Sloan.

'And zinnia,' said Margaret Sloan. 'You should have got that, Chris. You're the gardener.'

'And you're the cook,' he said. Canteens were no challenge to home cooking.

'Sorry. There's no more left. Bring young Crosby round one evening and I might make a steak and kidney pudding. It's not worth doing for only two.'

'When he's done a bit of work on this case.'

'What's all this about the letter "Z" then?'

He told her.

He was still talking about the case when his telephone rang.

Gregory Rosart had stayed on at the offices of Chernwoods' long enough to get Joe Keen's phone call.

'I'm not sure you were right, Greg, about squashing Claude's idea about a press release,' said the chief chemist.

Rosart bit back the obvious retort that it had been Keen who had been against it to start with. 'And what do you suggest?' he said with the self-control of the skilled public relations man.

'Had you thought that a little bit of publicity might

123

produce that woman you're looking for from way back?'

'Miss Catherine Camus?' guardedly. 'No, Joe, that hadn't occurred to me.'

'You never know what'll come out of the woodwork once the newspapers get going,' said Keen.

'Joe, do you think Harris and Marsh have stopped buying because they've got what they were looking for?'

'Perhaps, or . . .'

'Or?'

'Or they've dreamed up another way of getting it. Hadn't thought of that, had you?'

'No,' said Gregory Rosart thoughtfully. 'No, I hadn't.'

Amelia had made her way home through the dark streets more than satisfied with her evening's researches. With only a modicum of luck she soon should be able to find out exactly what the Fearnshires had been up to in those crucial months of March, May, and December 1940. And even perhaps glean from its history what its connection with a young Octavia Harquil-Grasset had been – although now she was beginning to think that she could work that out for herself.

Just as her great-aunt would have expected of her . . .

She would now start to look for someone called Kate and the location of the cross on the photograph Great-Aunt Octavia had so carefully left for her. After, that is, she had studied the regimental history of the Fearnshires. Tomorrow, too, she would go over her great-aunt's Will again. Since the old lady had taken such care with it there might be clues that had escaped her this morning – had it only been this morning? She hadn't really studied the Will properly either . . . what was that saying which had popped up in her history lectures? 'Documents don't speak to strangers' . . . she would look at the Will with new eyes in the morning . . .

Amelia turned into her own road, wondering if, after

all, Phoebe had got back from her clinical meeting before her . . . she herself had certainly been out for quite a time. She crossed the road behind a parked car. She pushed open the gate, noting only subconsciously that it was unlatched and that she remembered closing it carefully after her when she had gone out earlier in the evening.

Amelia turned her gaze towards the garage but its doors were shut and she couldn't tell at a glance whether her stepmother was back indoors or not. She started up the path . . . and nearly fell over something lying on the ground.

As she regained her balance she looked down more carefully.

She had almost fallen over the figure of a girl – a girl from the back of whose head was oozing something dark and sticky.

SIXTEEN

Plant his poor grave with whatever grows fast.

'Good grief, Sloan,' exploded Superintendent Leeyes, 'can't you even keep young girls safe at night in the streets of Berebury now?'

'This girl wasn't in the street, sir,' returned Sloan levelly. 'At least, not when she was found. She was in the garden of Amelia Kennerley's house. We don't know yet exactly where she was attacked.'

'By an unknown assailant, I suppose?' said the superintendent sourly.

'Unknown to us, sir,' conceded Sloan tacitly. 'We don't know whether he – or they – were unknown to her because she's still deeply unconscious and can't tell us.' Actually to Sloan the girl in the hospital had looked more like a lay figure than a living person.

Leeyes grunted as Sloan went on.

'Amelia Kennerley remembered noticing a small blue car parked in the road when she crossed it and that's all.'

'That's not much help.'

'Then her stepmother, Dr Plantin, arrived back from a medical meeting at Calleford. She dressed the girl's head wound while waiting for the ambulance and got her off to hospital.'

Leeyes grunted again.

'And neither she nor Dr Plantin knew the girl by sight,' said Sloan before he could ask.

'Does Tod Morton?' asked Leeyes, whose own Monday

night had been spent in bed undisturbed. 'He saw a girl.'

'We're getting him to go to the hospital to take a look-see,' said Sloan. 'She wasn't carrying anything to say who she was. We're going to get the rector of Great Primer to go up there, too, but I want to talk to him myself first.'

'You've set up a bed-watch on the girl, I trust.'

'I have, sir,' said Sloan, returning to his narrative. 'The girl was attacked from behind with something smooth and heavy about an hour before she was found and that's about all we can tell at the moment . . .'

'And, Sloan,' said the Superintendent acidly, 'do we know whether this girl was assaulted in her own right so to speak or in mistake for Amelia Kennerley?'

'No,' said Sloan frankly, 'we don't, but it's not as simple as that, sir.'

Leeyes groaned. 'I didn't think it would be. Go on . . .'

'We aren't sure why the girl was at the house anyway but—'

'Getting nowhere fast, then, aren't we?'

Detective Inspector Sloan said: 'Only in a manner of speaking, sir. But there is also the house . . .'

'This is no time for riddles, Sloan. You should know that. What do you mean?'

'Someone was doing there, sir, what I think they'd already done at the Grange last Friday.'

'Looking for something . . .'

'Just so, sir,' said Sloan wearily. His own night had not been spent undisturbed in bed. 'I think that they – whoever *they* may have been – can't have found what they were searching for at the Grange . . .'

'Whatever that might have been,' said Leeyes, whose highly idiosyncratic approach to algebra had never – without argument – got past the point of letting a equal one thing and b another. He was a little better about allowing the letter x stand for the unknown quantity: but not much.

'Whatever that might have been,' agreed Sloan, 'when they did over the Grange at Great Primer.' He went on more slowly: 'As they presumably didn't find what they wanted there, they may have therefore concluded that Mrs Garamond's solicitors might have had it . . .'

'Whatever it was . . .'

'Whatever it is,' said Sloan more hopefully, 'and decided that it wasn't likely to be easily accessible when locked in the solicitors' office safe but might be so if it had later been handed to Amelia Kennerley. As sole executrix, presumably she would have been entitled to have it, whatever it might be.'

'So,' suggested Leeyes, 'you think they turned her house over instead?'

'It would seem so.' Detective Inspector Sloan drew breath.

'But you still don't know what for, do you?' said Leeyes, putting an unerring finger on the weakness.

'No, we don't. As it happens, sir, the only item which James Puckle, the solicitor, had actually handed over to Amelia Kennerley was a rather blurred photograph of a wayside memorial.'

'Ah!'

Sloan couldn't remember the name of the man who had said 'But me no buts' but he felt a considerable fellow-feeling towards him, and would have liked himself to have said 'Ah me no ahs' to the superintendent but didn't think he should. There was, after all, his pension to think of . . .

Instead he said that as it happened Dr Phoebe had had the photograph safely in her handbag all afternoon and evening and if that was what the unknown intruder had been seeking then he hadn't got it because Dyson was working on the photograph in his darkroom at this very moment and had promised his report soonest.

He might have known that that wouldn't have been

quick enough for the superintendent who said: 'How, Sloan, can a photograph be as important as that?'

'I couldn't say, sir, I'm sure,' replied Sloan, who certainly wasn't going to attempt to explain anything about the possible significance of a regimental motto to a man who had once been heard to dismiss William Shakespeare's *Othello* as a lot of fuss over a handkerchief.

'I'll expect a situation report by noon then,' said the superintendent briskly. 'Well, man, what are you waiting for? Don't just stand there . . .'

Sloan coughed. 'I'm afraid, sir, that it appears that there is a slight complication in our listing of those who might have known about Miss Kennerley's having been appointed sole executrix.'

Beetle-browed, the superintendent said: 'Oh, there is, is there?'

'Apparently Mortons, the undertakers, have been giving it to anyone who asked.'

'No reason for them not to, I suppose,' said Leeyes grudgingly. 'It can't be kept secret for ever . . . so what, then, do you propose doing next, Sloan?'

A stranger listening to Superintendent Leeyes might have been misguided enough to think that he had performed a complete volte-face and was suddenly favouring the non-directive approach. Detective Inspector Sloan, who knew better, said: 'I'm going back to the hospital . . .'

Leeyes grunted.

'After which, sir, I'm going out to Great Primer to see Mr Fournier, which I think I should have done earlier. And then I shall try to see two old fellows called Nicholas Cochin and Martin Didot and look for an ancient lady by the name of Miss Catherine Camus.'

'Phoebe, when are you going to ring the hospital again?'

'I'm not,' responded Phoebe Plantin equably. 'They

129

won't tell anyone anything worthwhile over the telephone anyway. Besides, I must be off now.'

'That poor girl.' Amelia still looked stricken. 'It might have been me.'

Phoebe said soberly: 'It might have been meant to be you.'

They were standing together in the hallway of a house which had been searched at speed and left in disorder. 'The police say we can tidy up,' said Amelia. 'I'll get started on all this.'

'Better to have something to do,' agreed Phoebe, 'but I'd think twice about answering the door, all the same.'

Amelia started to restore order in the kitchen first – someone had even seen fit to examine the tea caddy – but she couldn't keep her mind on it. Impulsively she rang James Puckle and told him what had happened.

'Mr Puckle, I need to start looking for someone from the Fearnshires who was killed after Great-Aunt knew she was pregnant but before she could get married . . .'

'That will only give you the name of the child's father,' said Puckle, 'and then it would only be supposition . . .'

'It would be something.'

'It would help more if we knew the adoptive name given to their daughter,' countered Puckle, 'and, more-over, it is unlikely to explain the great interest that your great-aunt's former firm appear now to be taking in her effects, to say nothing of those who have broken and entered.'

'And injured,' she said, telling him of the unknown girl lying nigh unto death.

'Miss Kennerley,' he counselled earnestly, 'you must take care, great care. And I think you must also tell the police the terms of the precatory trust. You may be in great danger and that would have been the last thing Mrs Garamond wanted.'

'No,' she said harshly. 'The last thing she wanted was the police at her funeral. Remember?'

130

Her next telephone call was to a secondhand bookseller called Henryson.

The rector of Great Primer was in his garden trying to start his grass mower. He gave a final despairing pull at a recalcitrant two-stroke engine. It did not respond. Regarding the machine with savagery, the rector slowly straightened his back and asked the two policemen their business.

'Old Mrs Garamond?' he said, frowning. 'I took my letter round to the Grange about half-past four on Friday afternoon. After all, if they want a funeral service taken next Friday afternoon, and I am given to understand by the undertakers that they do, then I need to know the details, don't I?'

'Yes, rector. Naturally.'

'To say nothing of alerting the choristers and the bell-ringers . . . if they're going to be wanted, that is . . .'

'I couldn't say about that, sir,' began Sloan, saying nothing at all either about the very real possibility of his having to stop the funeral altogether for further enquiries to be made, 'but . . .'

'I dare say they will be,' said Mr Fournier grudgingly. He produced a large handkerchief and wiped his hands on it. He seemed slightly surprised when streaks of black oil appeared on the white linen and quickly stuffed it back into his pocket. 'That sort of person always likes to go out in style.'

'I can't say about that either,' said Sloan, 'but we would like to know a little more about who you saw when you delivered your letter to the Grange.'

'A girl walking back down the drive,' said Mr Fournier immediately. 'Away from the house. She was carrying a bunch of flowers.'

'Age?' The hospital had estimated their grey-faced, bandaged patient as twenty-four.

'Youngish.'

131

'Did you happen to notice what she was wearing?' Detective Inspector Sloan did not entirely subscribe to the view that clothes made the man, but they certainly helped in putting together a police description.

'A perfectly ordinary summer dress . . .'

An ordinary dress had been removed from the girl in hospital, only it wasn't perfect any longer.

'What did she say?' After all, thought Sloan, they weren't talking about a ghostly visitation but a live girl. The be-tubed girl in the hospital was alive so far . . . but the hospital had been very guarded.

'She told me that she had been very much hoping to see Mrs Garamond but there had been no reply at the Grange.'

'She wasn't carrying anything else . . . ?' The hospital patient had had no means of identification about her person.

'Not that I noticed, Inspector.' The rector explained that he had told her about Mrs Garamond's death.

'And how did she take the news?'

'She appeared to be most upset. She asked about relatives and I referred her to Mortons, the undertakers, since someone must have instructed them.'

'The last time, rector, that you saw Mrs Garamond, she didn't happen to mention that she was expecting visitors?'

'The last time I saw Mrs Garamond,' said the clergyman, who appeared to be nursing some kind of a grievance, 'all she would talk to me about were hatchments.'

Detective Inspector Sloan opened his mouth to speak but was thwarted.

'Hatchments, I ask you!' uttered the rector with unexpected violence. 'In this day and age with half the children in the world starving, the wealthiest woman in my parish insists on talking to me about a medieval anachronism like hatchments.'

'Quite so,' murmured Sloan, although from what he

remembered from his history lessons, surely it had been medieval people who had taken Christianity most seriously of all? 'Perhaps you would remind me about hatchments, rector?'

Mr Fournier sniffed. 'A custom, affected by those who think themselves a cut above their neighbours, of having a lozenge-shaped painted wooden tablet exhibiting the armorial bearings of the deceased affixed to the front of their last dwelling-place . . .'

'I see,' said Sloan. 'A sort of "Keeping up with the Joneses".'

'For a year after death,' continued the rector, 'after which it was customary for it to be received into the church, where it hangs for ever afterwards.'

'Or until Kingdom Come,' amplified Crosby, who had suddenly started to take an interest in the proceedings.

The rector was undeflected by this helpful theological comment and surged on indignantly: 'Not only couldn't I get her interested in aiding the starving children of the underdeveloped world, Inspector, but to my mind she didn't seem to care that the other half of the world – funnily enough – seems to be determined to destroy themselves and everyone else on this planet while they're about it.'

'Quarrelled with her about it, did you, sir?' asked the detective inspector. Doctrine wasn't his province: disagreement might be. Wealth was his concern more often than he liked.

'I suppose you could say that I took issue with her,' admitted the clergyman. He paused and then added significantly: 'Or she with me.'

'On the starving children of the underdeveloped world,' enquired Sloan gravely, 'or the hatchment?'

'Neither, Inspector.' The rector began to look even more heated. 'It was a matter of principle with me, Inspector, and thus no light matter.'

'What was?' asked Sloan at his most avuncular.

'Didn't you know, Inspector?' Mr Fournier stood erect beside the lawn mower and declared: 'The first point on which Mrs Garamond and I fundamentally disagreed was the keeping of Remembrance Sunday each November at the time nearest to the anniversary of Armistice Day.'

'Ah . . .'

'You see, Inspector, when I first came to this living two years ago I insisted on stopping the annual church parade and the two minutes' silence at eleven o'clock.'

'On principle?'

'Exactly. You know the sort of thing I mean, I'm sure. Martial music from old wars guaranteed to get people emotionally stirred up and a congregation who never sets foot in the church on any other Sunday in the year . . .'

There, divined Sloan silently, was the rub.

'Old men wearing old medals and carrying tattered flags . . . and children admiring them. That was what I didn't like. Glorifying war, that's all it was.'

Shakespeare – Sergeant Shakespeare, perhaps? – hadn't thought so, Sloan reminded himself, and old men certainly didn't forget.

The rector was still speaking. 'And I won, Inspector, even though Mrs Garamond went over my head to the Bishop of Calleford.' Ironically he squared his shoulders as he said: 'I may as well tell you that I'm an active pacifist and proud of it.'

'And the late Mrs Garamond wasn't?' ventured Sloan mildly.

'Certainly not. Do you know what she had the gall to quote to me once?'

'No,' said Sloan with genuine interest. He was beginning to feel even more curious about the late Octavia Garamond himself. In his experience middle-aged and overweight clergy seldom got excited about anything at all, but never about wilful old women.

' "*Dulce et decorum est pro patria mori*." ' The rector

pushed the lawnmower out of the way and stood facing the two policemen and said: 'Which, being translated' – Detective Constable Crosby's head came up at the mention of the word 'translated' – 'means,' carried on Mr Fournier, 'that "It is a sweet and fitting thing to die for one's country." '

'Very probably, sir,' said Sloan, in as neutral a tone as he could manage. Plenty of policemen died, too, in much the same cause – keeping the Queen's peace.

'Did you know,' remarked Detective Constable Crosby to no one in particular, 'that only a bishop gains by translation?'

'I must tell you,' said Mr Fournier, ignoring Crosby and pointing in the direction of a Georgian rectory which was large enough for a cleric with a quiverful of children, 'that I am a devoted supporter of any movement which leads to peace.'

Even at this distance Sloan could make out a symbol borrowed from the semaphore code above the door. 'And the late Mrs Garamond wasn't?' he deduced aloud, forbearing to draw any parallel with a hatchment on another dwelling-place.

'She was a very militant woman.' Edwin Fournier pressed his lips together into a thin, unamused line. 'Do you know what she once said to me?'

'No.' Sloan waited.

'That she thought a small war every now and then was a good thing for a nation. Kept the race on its toes, she said.'

Sloan coughed. 'I think you mentioned, rector, that your discontinuing the Remembrance Sunday service was only the first matter on which you had a disagreement with the dec— with the late Mrs Garamond?'

Mr Fournier's colour, already florid from the sun and unusual exertion, turned a shade still more puce. 'She took me to the consistory court . . .'

'Did she, indeed?' murmured Sloan. It was a court in which he had never given evidence. So far. 'What for?'

'Removing the War Memorial from the Lady Chapel without a faculty.' The rector said tonelessly, 'I lost.'

'Tell me,' said Sloan, a detective on duty, 'was there a member of her family commemorated there?'

'Not to my knowledge, Inspector.'

'So?'

'Had to get it put back as it was,' Edwin Fournier said, head down over the mower.

'I understand,' said Sloan, 'that nevertheless she asked particularly for you to take her funeral.'

'Wanted the last word, I suppose,' said the rector ungraciously. 'Difficult to the end, if you ask me.'

'If you ask me, sir,' said Detective Inspector Sloan, policeman first but gardener a close second, 'what that machine needs is . . .'

'Yes?' said the man of peace eagerly.

'A little less of the tickler and a bit more of the strangler.'

SEVENTEEN

Farewell, sweet ginger, dead in thy beauty.

Shirley Doves looked up from the basket of washing which she was hanging out in her back garden. 'Seen you before, haven't I?'

'You have,' said Detective Constable Crosby.

'Go on,' she said, gripping a clothes peg with her teeth. 'Say "once seen, never forgotten".'

'In a manner of speaking,' said Crosby, 'that's what I've come about.'

'Once seen, never forgotten? Get away.'

'The man in the Dog and Duck who made you a bit late at the Grange, Thursday night . . .'

'You still on about that?'

'Did you know him?'

Shirley Doves shook her head. Since she had added yet another clothes peg to her mouth the effect was macabre. 'Never seen 'im before. Nor since, come to that, seeing as the old lady's gone.'

'What were you drinking Thursday?'

Shirley pegged out two towels before she answered Crosby. 'I was on lager and lime and Ron was drinking bitter.'

'All the time?'

'Until this fellow asked us to celebrate with him. Just as we were going.'

'Celebrate what?'

Shirley Doves looked blank. 'Dunno. He just said he'd had a bit of luck and what would we like.'

137

'Go on,' said Crosby.

'Well,' she said glibly, watching his face, 'Ron was driving so he just had another bitter . . .'

'Drinking and driving's not my department,' he said sturdily.

'But this fellow asked what I really liked. It was a big celebration, he said, and I was to say whatever I wanted.'

'And you said . . ?'

'A whisky mac,' said Shirley Doves promptly. 'And blow me, that's what he bought me. I didn't think I should be so lucky.'

'What did he look like?'

'Ordinary sort of bloke.' She screwed up her eyes. 'Dressed a bit nunty perhaps, that's all . . .'

'Nunty?'

'You know – sort of old-fashioned, like.'

Crosby didn't know but conscientiously made an entry in his notebook.

'You going to the funeral, then?' he said.

'Course I am,' she said, affronted. 'I always go to my old ladies' funerals.'

Michael Harris sent for his director of finance on the Tuesday morning with something less than enthusiasm. Clever and hard-working the man might be, tactful he was not.

'Our broker tells me,' Harris said to him, 'that the price of Chernwoods' "A" Ordinary Shares has fallen back a bit since Friday.'

'Only to be expected,' responded David Gillsans. 'We weren't in the market yesterday and we're the only people who want to buy and why we do is beyond . . .'

'All right, all right.' Harris stayed him with his hand. 'It does mean that buying will be cheaper for us, though.'

'It means that there aren't quite so many other investors jumping on your take-over bandwagon as you might

138

have expected, that's all,' said Gillsans, adding privately that they had more sense.

Harris scratched his chin.

'And you can't buy any more shares now, whatever the price, without either declaring your intentions or breaking the law,' Gillsans added unequivocally. David Gillsans, as befitted an accountant, was a black and white man, not interested in a variety of shades of grey.

'I know, I know,' Harris said eagerly, 'but when we do come to buy over the limit it'll cost us less.'

Gillsans said tonelessly: 'That is one way of looking at the picture.'

'They may be worth a lot less by then, too . . .'

Gillsans looked up sharply but said nothing.

'A lot less,' said Harris craftily.

'The argument against buying at all remains the same,' said Gillsans.

'But you remember – the shares went down all right after they were up in court a couple of times.'

'That's only natural,' said Gillsans and stopped, deciding that if Harris was up to some mischief then he'd rather not know about it.

'Then I think,' said Harris mysteriously, 'that we should wait until next week before taking any further steps to buy.'

Gillsans nodded. Any time was too soon for him but next week was better than now. For once he wished that there was still a Marsh in the firm with whom he could have reasoned but the Marsh of Harris and Marsh's was as dead as Mr Scrooge's long gone partner, Jacob Marley.

'I shall be going to the funeral, of course,' said Harris, revealing what it was about this week that encouraged delay. 'I've arranged for a wreath to be sent . . .'

'I know,' said the accountant unkindly. 'They've charged it to the advertising budget.'

*

'It's very kind of you to come here, Mr Henryson . . .'

'Dr Phoebe's our doctor, Miss Kennerley,' said the bookseller obliquely, handing over a book. 'My wife won't see anyone else at the surgery.'

'But what about Undertones of War?'

He gave her a deprecating smile. 'My customers don't mind having to come back, you know. They're enthusiasts and time doesn't matter too much to them. Besides,' he bowed his head, 'you said it was important.'

'It is.' Amelia said: 'It may seem silly, Mr Henryson, but I do really need to know the names of the soldiers in the Fearnshires who were killed in the last war, probably in 1940.'

'Ah, then I think this will help you.' The bookseller opened the book. 'Their regimental history . . .'

'Marvellous! Do let me see . . .'

'The Fearnshires had rather a bad time in France in 1940,' said Mr Henryson. 'After the fall of France,' said Mr Henryson, 'the 2nd Battalion were trapped between two advancing German forces. They were far too far south, you see, to make for Dunkirk . . .'

'Where they might have got away.' Amelia had that epic firmly in her mind.

'They might,' agreed Mr Henryson. 'They might possibly have been trying to break through to St Valery-en-Caux – they were hoping at one time to evacuate some men from there . . .'

'They didn't, though, did they?'

Mr Henryson shook his head. 'No. The Fearnshires held out for as long as they could, of course' – there was a wealth of military meaning in that *of course* – 'but in the end . . .'

'Yes?'

The military bookseller said: 'Superior forces prevailed . . .'

'As they usually do,' said Amelia logically.

'Not always,' said Mr Henryson, amateur historian. 'There were David and Goliath, you know. However, I fear the 2nd Battalion of the Fearnshires were either killed or taken prisoner at a village called Hautchamps.' Mr Henryson pointed to the volume he'd brought. 'It's all in that history there. A little place called Hautchamps is where they made their last stand.'

'Is there a memorial there?' Amelia opened the history and began to turn the pages.

Mr Henryson said he was pretty sure that there would be, and there was certainly another in the form of a Scottish cairn at their battalion headquarters because he'd seen it.

A big one.

He was sure, he said, that she knew the origin of the cairn as a memorial and the significance of its size.

'The bigger the battle, the bigger the cairn?' hazarded Amelia with half her mind, turning the pages of the history as quickly as she could.

'Not quite,' said Mr Henryson. 'It dates from the days before muster rolls . . .'

The Fearnshires, decided Amelia, would seem to have had cannon to the right of them and cannon to the left of them in that dreadful Maytime.

'When a Highlander leaving for a battle left a stone on a pile before he went,' continued the bookseller, 'and . . .'

The Fearnshires, read Amelia, had had trouble defending their rear, too.

'And,' said the indefatigable Mr Henryson, 'when – if – the soldier came back home he collected his stone. So the greater the pile of unclaimed stones, the greater the number of casualties . . .'

Amelia interrupted his disquisition. 'Mr Henryson, what does "enfiladed" mean?'

'Fire from artillery which sweeps a line of men or buildings from end to end,' responded Mr Henryson promptly.

'I thought it might,' said Amelia, suddenly sad. She read out: ' "On the evening of 10th June 1940, the men were rallied and reformed at the Hautchamps crossroads by Second Lieutenant E. H. Goudy of the 2nd Battalion, the Fearnshires, after being raked by enemy fire." '

'*Nec temere, nec timide*,' observed Mr Henryson. 'That was what you were looking for, wasn't it?'

Amelia read on. ' "Second Lieutenant Goudy was among those killed by mortar fire at first light the next morning." '

The bookseller looked at her. 'Is that who you were looking for?'

Amelia blinked away a sudden mist in her eyes and nodded without speaking.

'Battles long ago and far away are best,' offered Mr Henryson, although he didn't think she was listening.

Mr Nicholas Cochin lived in Calleford in a bungalow on the edge of the town. The two policemen found his house without difficulty. There was just the one impediment to interviewing him and that was that he and his wife were in Canada visiting a married daughter.

Their next-door neighbour had undertaken the care of their house plants and the forwarding of mail. He told Sloan that there had indeed been other callers at the house, to whom they had given the same information but no more than this.

No, the other callers had not given their names . . . but had said that they would pay another visit when the Cochins were back home again.

No, the neighbour couldn't describe any of them.

The police fared rather better with their next call.

Martin Didot lived in Luston in his retirement and was a spry old man with all his wits still about him. Though he was old he was not yet really old nor what the geriatricians fashionably now call old, old.

'Chernwoods' in the war, Inspector? Yes, I worked there all right. Man and boy, you might say. That was when the last of the Chernwood family were still there. They were great days, you know. It was never the same after the new management took over.'

'No, sir, I'm sure, but . . .'

'They were in the papers a while back when someone sued them for wrongful dismissal.' He regarded Sloan straightly and said severely: 'That sort of thing would never have happened in the old days, you know. It's not good for a firm, that sort of thing.'

'No, sir,' agreed Sloan, 'it isn't.'

'And then, not so long ago, they had a fire.'

'That was bad luck,' said Sloan.

'If you ask me,' said Didot, 'it was arson.'

'Was it now . . .' Sloan made a mental note to look into that later.

'I went down the next morning to have a look at the old place myself. Works were a right mess and swarming with fire scientists and insurance assessors . . .'

Detective Inspector Sloan made yet another note in his book.

'Seems to me, lad,' said Didot, 'that there's someone wanting to do the old firm an injury . . .'

'What I've come to ask you, sir,' said Detective Inspector Sloan briskly (he hadn't been called 'lad' for many a long year), 'is something about Hut Eleven.'

Sloan found himself being surveyed by a remarkably shrewd – if rheumy – pair of eyes. He said quizzically: 'You, too, Inspector?'

'There have been others, then?'

'Oh, yes,' he nodded, 'there have been others. From the management and from who knows where. And . . .'

'And?'

'They all want to know what we were doing in Hut Eleven then.'

143

Sloan leaned forward. 'And what do you tell them, Mr Didot?'

'The truth, Inspector. That I was only the lab boy there. Then they usually go away.'

'But you knew about OZ?' persisted Sloan, who wasn't going to go away.

'I knew about it, Inspector, but that's all.'

'Go on.'

'That is to say, I knew about it to the extent of being able to say I knew that there was research being done under that name but not exactly what it was.' He looked out of the window. 'It was all a very long time ago, now, you know.'

'That is one of the difficulties,' said Sloan, undeterred. The long arm of the law had reached backwards before now. And further.

'And,' Didot said in a matter-of-fact way, 'I wasn't educated like the others were. They were mostly trained scientists, you know, recruited straight from the universities as soon as the war got going.'

'Mrs Garamond knew all about it, though, didn't she?' suggested Sloan. The neat little terraced house, polished to perfection, seemed totally remote from war-time research into anything.

'Oh, yes, but then it was her discovery, wasn't it?'

'What was?' asked Sloan quietly.

'OZ,' said Martin Didot, 'you know, Inspector, Operation Zenith . . .'

'No, I didn't know. Tell me, what was Operation Zenith, Mr Didot?'

'Like I said, Inspector, I don't know. I was only the lab boy helping with getting apparatus ready for the others.' He stared into nothing, his mind going back. 'But it was important, I can tell you that.'

'More important,' said Sloan, 'than Operation Tell-tale?'

'Much more important.'

'Where would I find it?'

'You won't, Inspector. Not now that Rikki-Tikki-Tavi's gone. That's what we used to call Mrs Garamond behind her back, you know. She was great.'

'Who would still know?'

'Like I said, no one.' Martin Didot paused for thought. 'No. There aren't many of us old 'uns left now.'

'What about Nicholas Cochin?'

Martin Didot sniffed expressively. 'He always acted as if he knew but I don't think he did really. Bit of a show-off was our Nicholas. Clever-clogs was what we called him behind his back.'

Detective Inspector Sloan, who knew the value of silence better than most men, waited.

Eventually the man went on: 'I suppose the only people left now who might know would be Alfred Harris and Miss Camus . . .'

'Miss Kate Camus?' It was the last name on Sloan's list.

Didot looked knowingly at Sloan and rubbed the side of his nose. 'If you ask me, she was a bit sweet on William Garamond but it was Rikki-Tikki-Tavi who he married.'

Sloan said urgently: 'Where would I find Miss Camus, Mr Didot?'

'Nobody knows that, Inspector. She left Chernwoods' just after the war and hasn't been heard from since. Didn't you know?'

'That you, Sloan? Dabbe here. Where the devil have you been?'

'Out and about,' said Sloan truthfully. 'And here and there . . . trying to identify an unconscious girl mostly.'

'Well,' said Dabbe, who was seldom concerned with the living, 'I've just been talking to my old friend Stony Agate. You remember – the forensic toxicologist I told you about.'

'I remember,' said Sloan. 'You met over a dead leg.'

'Well, he's pretty sure that that old lady of yours . . .'

Mrs Octavia Garamond was every bit the pathologist's case, too, but Sloan didn't say so. 'Yes?' he invited.

'Stony, that's what we called Agate – I did tell you that, Sloan, didn't I?'

'Yes, doctor . . .'

'Well, Stony says . . .'

There had been a game that Sloan had played when young called 'Simon says . . .' He must remember to teach it to his son. If, that is, if he ever got home before the boy went to bed.

'Stony now says he thinks the deceased probably died from inhaling a vapour . . .'

Detective Inspector Sloan's head came up. 'A vapour, doctor?'

'Well, gas if you'd rather . . .'

'Poison gas?'

'Fumes given off by adding sodium hydroxide to ethylene chlorhydrin,' said Dr Dabbe down the telephone.

'But how on earth could anyone have got toxic fumes into the old lady's lungs?' asked Sloan. There had been nothing but oxygen in the cylinder by Mrs Garamond's bed; that had been checked.

'Stony says you put your ethylene chlorhydrin into an alembic flask first . . .'

'First catch your ethylene chlorhydrin, surely . . .' said Sloan, who thought catching a hare would have been easier by half.

'Not difficult,' said Dr Dabbe. 'It's stable and cheap . . .'

'All right,' capitulated Sloan, 'then what?'

'Then, when you've got it under the victim's nose all you have to do is to add some sodium hydroxide and – er – Bob's your uncle. Or, more precisely,' said Dr Dabbe, 'what you might say is that it would be curtains for anyone breathing in the result. I say, Sloan,' he added, 'do you think "curtains" became a synonym for death because of the curtains in the crematorium or because they were drawn on stage after a play? "The rest is silence" and all that?'

'The result?' asked Sloan, pertinaceous policeman that he was. He thought that curtains had come to mean death because they used to be drawn when someone in the house had died. His grandmother had told him that – his grandmother and Wilfred Owen's 'And each slow dusk a drawing-down of blinds . . .' He said again, 'What result, doctor?'

'The result of mixing sodium hydroxide with ethylene chlorhydrin,' responded the pathologist, 'chemically, will be ethylene oxide.'

'Will it?' said Sloan, more than a little uncertain of the spelling of what he should be getting down on paper.

'And, Sloan, the important thing about ethylene oxide from your point of view . . .'

'Yes?'

'Is that it becomes a gas at ordinary temperatures.'

'That's important, is it, doctor?' he said cautiously, wondering if he ought to ask the pathologist to spell 'chlorhydrin' for him or wait until the report came. The superintendent would be sure to ask.

'Well, that and the fact that it's fatal for whoever inhales it, of course. Neat, isn't it?' said Dr Dabbe. 'Stony's most interested – he doesn't think it's been done before.'

'I hope not,' said Sloan repressively.

'But he's pretty sure,' said Dabbe. 'Good chap, Stony. After dissecting that leg we went on to . . .'

'How sure?' enquired Sloan quickly.

'Expert witness sure,' said Dabbe concisely.

'Ah . . .' said Sloan, relieved. That meant that the pathologist's friend didn't mind being cross-examined in the witness box by all comers.

'Actually,' confided the pathologist, 'he's rather looking forward to it. He likes murder trials.'

147

'Quite so,' said Sloan, 'but first I've – er – got to catch my hare.'

'Good hunting.'

'Come to that, doctor, I've got to catch a missing heir, too – or, rather, heiress – of the old lady for the executrix,' said Sloan. 'Amelia Kennerley now tells me that there's an illegitimate daughter unaccounted for, who's a possible legatee into the bargain.'

'Say on, Sloan . . .'

'She'd be in her fifties now, if still alive, and,' he went on, 'I've still got to establish who this head-injury girl is . . .'

There was a small silence at the other end of the telephone line and then Dr Dabbe said with quite uncharacteristic diffidence: 'You couldn't send me round some of her hair, could you, Sloan? Just a few strands . . .'

EIGHTEEN

Silent through summer, though other birds sing

In their separate ways both Police Superintendent Leeyes and Detective Constable Crosby had some difficulty in coming to terms with Detective Inspector Sloan's behaviour on the Wednesday morning.

He spent it sitting at his desk in his office.

Detective Constable Crosby was the first to disturb his reverie.

'Where to this morning, sir?' he asked from the door, car-keys at the ready.

'Nowhere,' said Sloan, ignoring a pile of reports on his desk. 'Oh, Crosby, you could go and check that nothing more on the whereabouts of Miss Kate Camus has come in.'

'If she was important, sir, wouldn't the old lady have had her address?'

'Perhaps, Crosby. And if wishes were horses, beggars could ride.'

'Sir?' He sounded injured.

'One, we don't know that Miss Kate Camus remained unmarried – she could be Mrs Anybody for all we know – and two, Mrs Garamond's address book, if she had one, isn't at the Grange any more. We checked.'

'Stolen?'

'Very probably.'

'To stop us finding her?'

'Or to enable others to find her.'

'First?'

'That is among my worries, Crosby.'

'Yes, sir.'

'The fact that Miss Camus was of an age to be working during the last war means that she, too, will no longer be young.'

'If she's still alive,' said Crosby.

'But,' pronounced Sloan, 'the fact that if she is alive she will now be old does not mean that she is not entitled to live out her days as she wishes rather than have them truncated by violence as would seem to have happened in the case of Octavia Garamond.' Sloan waved a report in his hand. 'Dr Dabbe and his friend Professor Agate seem sure that Mrs Garamond was murdered.'

'Yes, sir. So am I.'

Sloan looked up, surprised. 'You are, are you? Why so sure?'

'Men in pubs don't ask total strangers to drink with them by way of a celebration at the end of the evening,' said Crosby simply. 'It's not natural. They'd do it when they first came in, wouldn't they? Stands to reason.'

'True,' agreed Sloan. Perhaps they'd make a detective of Crosby one day after all.

'I reckon, sir, that he slipped Mrs Shirley Doves a Micky Finn so she'd sleep extra well that night.'

'Then you'd better check on how the description of your stranger with something to celebrate jibes with that of all the other males in the case. Except the doctor. Mrs Doves knew him.'

'Yes, sir,' said Crosby, jangling the car-keys hopefully. 'And then?'

'And then you can come and help me with some paper-work,' said Sloan, thus ensuring a prolonged absence on Crosby's part. 'I'm going to be working on two lists – what we know and what we don't know.'

'Yes, sir.'

'And one list is a good deal longer than the other . . .'

'Yes, sir.'

'In fact, what we know would go on one side of a piece of paper.'

'We do know there's something that someone's looking quite hard for,' said Crosby. 'And small.'

'But not what it is.'

'Something pretty valuable, though, sir, or there wouldn't have been all this fuss.'

'If by "fuss", Crosby, you mean murder, then yes, valuable to someone.'

'But we don't know who, do we, sir?'

'Chernwoods' Dyestuffs, perhaps.'

'Or someone there,' said Crosby, who had difficulty in grasping the concept of corporate identity. Or responsibility.

'And Harris and Marsh's,' said Sloan.

'Or someone there, too,' said Crosby.

'But what we don't yet know,' he said, 'is whether something is being sought with a view to suppressing it . . .'

'Like those ever-lasting electric light bulbs that they're always on about?'

'Just like that,' agreed Sloan. 'Or whether what they are looking for is something that they could exploit.'

'Even if it's not theirs?' said Crosby.

Detective Inspector Sloan said: 'If the discovery was made at Chernwoods' by people on the staff there when they made it, then I should have thought that it belonged to Chernwoods'. Which might account for Harris and Marsh's wanting to buy them so badly.'

'Yes, sir.'

'They call them intellectual property rights these days but in the old days it was likely to be known as copyright or patent.'

Crosby's brow cleared. 'I see, sir. And so if Harris and

Marsh's did take over Chernwood's then it would be theirs instead to do what they liked with?'

'You've got it in one, Crosby,' said Sloan, mellowly, privately hoping that the superintendent could – and would – follow the same line of reasoning without too much argument.

'So what's this Miss Camus got to do with it?'

'My guess,' said Detective Inspector Sloan, 'is that Miss Kate Camus is now the only person alive who can tell us or anybody else what all this is about.' He amended this just as the telephone began to ring. 'Miss Camus and Dr Dabbe . . .'

'This funeral on Friday afternoon, Sloan,' began Leeyes as soon as that luckless officer put his head round the police superintendent's door. 'Do you want it stopped?'

'No, thank you, sir,' said Sloan politely.

'No?' A pair of bushy eyebrows shot up.

'No – I mean, Friday afternoon will do very well, thank you, sir.'

'Even though our friendly neighbourhood pathologist says it's a murder case?'

'Yes, sir. Especially because of that. He says he has all he needs for the Coroner.'

'And you've listed everyone with the knowledge that pouring one of these chemicals on to another would produce something nasty?'

'I have,' said Sloan. 'It's a long one. Including her doctor,' he added meticulously. 'Mrs Octavia Garamond was murdered by someone knowledgeable about chemistry.' He forbore to say in this case this was a factor which widened the field of suspects, rather than narrowed it.

'You're not hoping, Sloan, are you,' Leeyes boomed sarcastically, 'that the days of miracles are not yet over and that someone will find the occasion of the funeral emotionally too much for them and stand up and confess?'

152

'No, sir, but I would like Woman Police Sergeant Perkins out there at Great Primer on Friday.'

'Need your hand holding, do you?'

'I need a woman there,' said Sloan seriously, adding, 'and not in uniform.'

'Disguised as what?' Leeyes asked.

'A newspaper reporter from the *Luston News*.'

Leeyes grunted. 'That shouldn't be too difficult for Pretty Polly Perkins.'

'No, sir.' Sloan was confident that on Friday afternoon Woman Police Sergeant Perkins, if asked, would look every inch the provincial newspaper reporter.

'And this girl in hospital?'

'Not too good, sir.'

'That means hanging by a thread, I suppose.' Leeyes interpreted the hospital report with ease.

'She hasn't come round at all.'

'And you still don't know who she is?'

'Not yet.'

'So . . .'

'So, sir, we're going on with our search for an old lady called Kate Camus, last heard of just after the end of the war when she left Chernwoods' Dyestuffs, destination unknown.'

'It's an uncommon name.'

'She may have changed it, of course.'

'She may be dead.'

'Yes, sir.'

Leeyes said: 'And she may not know anything useful.'

'True, sir.' He coughed. 'Or she may have been murdered, too, but somehow I don't think so.'

'All right, all right, Sloan. I'll buy it. Why don't you think she's been murdered like Mrs Garamond?'

'Because,' said Sloan soberly, 'she can't be found.'

'And can we find her?'

'We're trying very hard, sir. We're pulling out all the

stops but we may not be the only people looking. That's the trouble.'

'Come home and be killed?'

'Something like that, sir.' He added slowly: 'I wouldn't like us to have done the finding and then have someone else do the killing.'

'So?'

'So I'm – er – holding my horses until the funeral.'

Claude Miller was not so much holding his horses for the funeral as limbering up. He soon sent for his information officer and librarian.

'Greg, I think I told you I'd offered to say a few words at Mrs Garamond's funeral.'

'You did,' said Rosart, without any noticeable enthusiasm.

'I'll need some background material.'

'Yes, Mr Miller. I'll dig out some facts for you. Dates and so forth.'

'I hear that Michael Harris is going to be there.' The girl on their switchboard and her cousin at Harris and Marsh's had proved invaluable sources of information when the two principals were officially only communicating through their solicitors.

'Our Michael wouldn't want to miss an occasion like that,' agreed Rosart, 'to say nothing of getting his name in the papers.'

'After all,' said Miller, already straightening his tie, 'the old lady was one of the jewels in Chernwoods' crown in the old days . . .'

'I think something a little more factual would be more in order, Mr Miller, when you actually speak.'

'Right,' said the chairman in what he liked to think were tones of command. 'You go ahead and put something on paper for me and I'll get in touch with the family . . .'

'Family?' Greg Rosart started. 'There's just the great-niece that I know about.'

'That's right. I say, Greg, what about a shot of us all going into the church? Or coming out? Do you think you could lay it on? Just for the record, of course . . .'

NINETEEN

Bury him comrades, in pitiful duty.

The men carrying the coffin on the Friday – Tod Morton's men – paused as in days of yore at the lich-gate of St Hilary's church at Great Primer while two large wreaths were placed on it. One was of red roses and the other of white and Amelia had chosen the colours.

The lich-gate where the cortège had halted had provided shelter and somewhere to sit in olden times when the cortège – without benefit of clock or writing – had had to wait upon the arrival of the cleric to take the burial service.

It wasn't like that any more.

The Reverend Edwin Fournier was already present, robed and cloaked, awaiting the coffin and ready to greet the mourners with what Amelia always thought of as 'comfortable words'.

What was not so comfortable was the knowledge that behind the immemorial churchyard yews there lurked men who were not mourners but policemen. Before Christianity the yew, then almost the only evergreen tree in England, had been a symbol of everlasting life in its own account. Today those yews in this country churchyard were providing cover for plain-clothes detectives on watch.

'Right, miss,' said Tod Morton, touching Amelia's shoulder. 'We're ready now.'

The crunch of feet in unison on gravel was all that

Amelia actually heard but her head was full of sounds and images and she felt a good deal more shakiness about the legs than she would have admitted to – even to Phoebe.

As the cortège entered the church the well-built lady from the newspaper finished her taking of names in the church porch – an old-fashioned custom of which no doubt Great-Aunt Octavia would have approved – and found herself a seat at the back of the church.

Detective Inspector Sloan had heeded the superintendent's advice and was somewhere near the back at the other side of the church. For reasons known only to the constabulary, Detective Constable Crosby was seated very near the front at the end of the side pew nearest to the vestry door.

It took Amelia a moment or two to adjust her eyes to the relative dimness inside the church after the bright sunlight of the churchyard. She blinked and then followed the little procession up the aisle. Tod Morton ushered her to the front pew and the Reverend Edwin Fournier began the Order of Service for the Burial of the Dead.

Before very long Amelia Kennerley found what countless others before her had done, that the front pew was not a good vantage point from which to study the congregation. She did, however, have from where she sat a very good view of the Lady Chapel. The names on the war memorial there – bitter bone of contention that it had been between priest and parishioner – were of men of the East Calleshire Regiment but there was no doubt in Amelia's mind now that it was a certain Second Lieutenant E. H. Goudy of the ill-fated Fearnshires whom Great-Aunt Octavia had had in mind when she knelt there. Not, from all accounts, that her marriage to her own mother's uncle William Garamond had been unhappy.

Just different, probably.

'We bring nothing into this world,' declared the Rever-

157

end Edwin Fournier to the assembled congregation, 'and it is certain that we carry nothing out . . .'

But, thought Amelia to herself, though Great-Aunt Octavia might have known that there are no pockets in a shroud, she had left her instructions for those who came after in no uncertain manner.

Detective Inspector Sloan swept the congregation with his gaze. He'd only met the eye of Woman Police Sergeant Perkins once but it had been enough. She had indicated a little old lady, grey-haired and nondescript, who had made her own way to a seat half-way down the centre aisle, and who sat now, alert and attentive to the reading.

It was from Ecclesiastes. ' "To everything",' read the rector, ' "there is a season, and a time to every purpose under the heaven . . ." '

Amelia sat upright, letting the words flow over her like balm.

' "A time to be born and a time to die",' read on the rector. ' "A time to plant and a time to pluck up that which is planted; a time to kill . . ." '

Detective Inspector Sloan was sitting stiffly upright in his pew, too, and wondering why there had been an exact time for someone to kill Mrs Garamond, giving thanks the while that the eyelids of an unconscious girl in the Berebury Hospital had begun to flicker. There was always a time to hope, too.

' "And a time to heal",' continued the rector, ' "a time to break down . . ." '

Octavia Harquil-Grasset hadn't broken down, thought Amelia in the front pew. She'd had her baby, mourned its father, handed her little daughter over for adoption, and gone to play her own part in the war effort.

' "A time to keep silence, and a time to speak; a time to love . . . and a time to hate . . ." '

Amelia wished she'd known her great-aunt, really

known her, that is. Not just as a Sunday afternoon visitor but known her well enough to know what she had really thought about things . . .

Edwin Fournier's voice went on above her thoughts. ' "A time of war . . ." '

That applied to Octavia Garamond, all right, decided Amelia.

' "And a time of peace",' concluded the rector firmly, closing the Bible and making his way back to his stall.

That, too, thought Amelia, as Claude Miller said his lapidary piece and the burial service wound its way to a conclusion.

Detective Inspector Sloan had had a longer time to look around the church and had a better vantage point from the back pew anyway. His role now he felt was the triple one, shared with a sheepdog, of at the one and the same time protecting the strays in his flock from danger, steering them in the direction in which he wanted them to go, and marking the goats in their midst.

Still inside the body of the church was Woman Police Sergeant Perkins, whose sole duty today was shadowing the little old lady who had given her name at the door as Miss Catherine Camus. Detective Constable Crosby had mysteriously slipped out of the vestry door and was standing in the churchyard right behind Mrs Shirley Doves, care assistant.

'Oh, yes,' she said, pointing. 'That's him, all right. He was the one in the Dog and Duck that night. Know him anywhere, I would.'

TWENTY

Muffle the dinner-bell, mournfully ring.

It was not the first time in the long history of that legal establishment that the offices of Puckle, Puckle, and Nunnery down by the bridge in Berebury had been the venue for explanation. It even occurred to Amelia Kennerley that her Great-Aunt Octavia would have felt the mahogany and the old worn leather to have made the setting even more appropriate.

The person who fitted into the old-fashioned surroundings best of all was Miss Kate Camus. She was a neat, rather prim-looking old lady who settled herself into one of James Puckle's chairs with complete composure.

'I can quite see your difficulty, Inspector,' she said to Sloan. 'The murderer must have come from either Chernwoods' Dyestuffs or Harris and Marsh's Chemicals . . .'

'I don't see why,' said Amelia, who had almost – but not quite – recovered from seeing the arrest of Gregory Rosart minutes after the committal of her great-aunt's body to the grave three days before.

'They were the only people who could have known about OZ,' said Miss Camus calmly. 'Chernwoods' from finding traces in their records – although we were very careful – and Harris and Marsh's from things that Albert Harris had said after he lost his wits.' She said: 'I went to see him yesterday and he's completely cuckoo, you know.'

160

'Yes,' said Detective Inspector Sloan, 'but his son isn't.' He'd just given Michael Harris the roughest hour of that opportunist's life before telling him that the police wouldn't be bringing charges for what the man in the street would have called insider trading even if the law didn't.

'What I don't quite see,' put in James Puckle, 'is why Rosart told you as much as he did . . .'

Surprisingly it was Detective Constable Crosby who answered him. 'He was trying to make patsies of us.' He was still smarting from the thought. 'Rosart couldn't find this lady here and he thought we could find her for him.'

'And,' added Kate Camus, 'he also made the mistake of thinking that if he found me, he'd get hold of OZ.'

'The secret of Hut Eleven?' said Amelia, wishing it didn't sound like the title of a bad children's book.

'One of them, anyway,' said Miss Camus.

James Puckle picked up the earlier point. 'It wouldn't have helped him, then, if Rosart had got to you first?'

'It might have stopped him hitting Jane Baskerville . . .' said Miss Camus with vigour.

'In mistake for me,' said Amelia. Rosart had vouchsafed that much. 'She happened on him leaving after the burglary.' The girl in Berebury Hospital had recovered consciousness long enough to tell them that. And more.

'This discovery,' said Sloan tenaciously keeping to the point, 'was it valuable?'

'It was a very important finding, Inspector,' said Miss Camus. 'Undoubtedly Operation Zenith was a real mile-stone in the biological sciences by any of the standards prevailing at the time.'

'Made by . . .'

'Oh, by Octavia Harquil-Grasset.' She shook her head. 'Not me.'

'What became of it?' he asked, although he was begin-ning to think he knew.

'We destroyed it,' she said serenely.

'Who did?'

'Tavi, Bill Garamond, and I.'

Detective Inspector Sloan said quietly: 'Would you tell us why?'

'Tavi didn't think the world was ready for it yet.'

'Miss Camus.' James Puckle spoke as a man of law should, slowly and carefully. 'Are you telling me that you and Mr and Mrs Garamond deliberately disposed of all the records of Hut Eleven?'

'Only of this one discovery, Mr Puckle,' she said, equally precisely. 'Not of any of our other work.'

'But,' put in Detective Inspector Sloan, policeman, 'every record of the discovery that was codenamed Operation Zenith?'

'Every single one, Inspector.' Miss Camus sounded completely matter of fact.

'Oh,' burst out Amelia, 'please tell us why . . .'

'Tavi was worried that if anyone else ever knew about it, it would eventually get into the wrong hands.' She surveyed her audience from the distance of old age and said: 'There was a very real danger then, you know, that England might still have been invaded.'

'But you knew what it was?' persisted Amelia. 'This discovery . . .'

Miss Camus adjusted her glasses and said precisely: 'I knew exactly what it was that Tavi had stumbled on – the nature of her discovery, so to speak. I did not know how she had done so and she did not tell me – in fact, I asked her not to do so in the interests of greater security.'

'But,' said Sloan, still sticking to the main issue, 'you agreed with her about its total destruction.'

'Oh, yes, indeed, I did. Who knows what dreadful misuse would have been made of it?' She regarded her audience and said: 'Don't forget that there was a war on

162

then in which the sciences were being put to purposes over which scientists had no control. Irreparable damage might have been done before anyone could stop it.' She looked unseeingly into the distance as she said: 'You're all too young to remember and being told isn't the same thing, I know, but there was an organized wickedness abroad in those days . . .'

'But tell us what it was,' pleaded Amelia. 'All I know is that my great-aunt had been working before on the way in which cells divide in plants . . .'

'What we at Chernwoods' were doing rather followed on from that,' said Kate Camus. 'We'd been looking at the possible uses in wartime of chemical dyes in and on human beings . . .'

'Operation Tell-tale . . .' said Sloan.

Miss Camus said with apparent irrelevance: 'Tavi had a very good brain, you know, and a lot of other interests besides the biological sciences. Psychology was one of her pet hobbies. She was a great reader of Sigmund Freud . . .'

'And?' said Sloan.

'And she thought she had come across under her microscope something that he had written about but not known how to identify.'

'She did, did she?' said Sloan. The name of Sigmund Freud was altogether too well known to them down at the police station. Especially his pleasure principle.

'But what was it?' cried Amelia.

'What Freud had called "the secret hour of life's midday",' said Miss Camus. 'That is barring accidents, naturally.'

The Detective Inspector heard himself echoing the old lady. 'Naturally.'

Miss Camus said hortatively: 'Tavi found a set of cells in some plants she had been working on which started to decline exactly half-way through the plant's life-cycle so she reasoned that animals might have a similar marker in their make-up.'

'And they did?' Sloan grasped the idea. Like all good ones, it was breathtakingly simple.

Miss Camus nodded. 'She went on to mice and . . . er . . . herself. The human body does replicate some animal species, you know.'

They knew that to their cost down at the police station, too. Bulls and boars, mostly.

It was the solicitor who spoke next. 'It would never have done,' said James Puckle, 'not for people to have known exactly when they were half-way through their lives.'

She smiled. 'That's what we thought, too.'

'It would have been a secret worth having, though,' murmured Sloan.

'Miss Camus,' said Amelia Kennerley impulsively, 'my great-aunt's Will said she "left a candle for Kate". Do you know why?'

'Ah.' A flush of real pleasure suffused the old lady's face, and for the first time Miss Kate Camus was apparently at a loss for words. When at last she found her voice she said with a catch in it: 'Now, that's a secret of Hut Eleven that I'm not going to tell you about . . . let's just say it's to do with an old flame.'

'You haven't left any loose ends, have you, Sloan?' said Superintendent Leeyes, who could probably have taught Sigmund Freud a thing or two about keeping the upper hand.

'No, sir. Mrs Garamond's discovery would have been a secret worth having, though,' said Sloan, conscious that it was only true sportsmen who thought it improper to bet on certainties, never actuaries or insurance companies.

'I'm not surprised,' said Leeyes acidly, 'considering how reluctant the medical profession has always been to

164

venture an opinion on when someone is going to die even when they do know.'

'The potential implications of her findings would have been very considerable,' agreed Sloan, adding 'to mankind in general and Chernwoods' Dyestuffs in particular.'

'What had Rosart in mind, then?'

'He wanted to be an important part of a management buy-out being led by Chernwoods' chief chemist.' Sloan opened his notebook. 'We realized that all the misfortunes which had beset the firm could have been engineered from within to keep the shares down. What spoilt that little plan was Harris and Marsh's Chemicals trying a take-over on their own account and bumping the share prices up again.'

'Huh.'

'They thought Chernwoods' held the secret of Hut Eleven without knowing they'd got it.'

'And that, I suppose, came of listening to old boy Harris's wanderings?'

'Yes, sir.'

'There're no holds barred in business, are there?' marvelled Leeyes.

'Red in tooth and claw, sir.' He said: 'I think we'll find Rosart got his ethylene chlorhydrin from somewhere in Chernwoods' but not from Keen.'

'And Harris and Marsh's . . . they just catch a cold, do they?' said Leeyes, whose own grasp of business finance was tenuous.

'Well, yes and no, sir.'

'And what is that supposed to mean?'

'Our man in the City, sir,' quoted Sloan, 'says that they'll probably have to merge with Chernwoods' Dyestuffs or go under.' It had sounded like a punishment worse than death to Sloan. 'And have their chief chemist on the board.'

'And the girl with the head injuries?'

'Jane Baskerville's holding her own very well, sir,' said Sloan, adding a garden aphorism: 'It's the rootstock that controls the vigour of the growth and we know that's all right.'

'And,' said the superintendent, undiverted, 'where does she come in, then?'

'Jane Baskerville is Mrs Garamond's granddaughter, sir.'

'So she says,' said Leeyes derisively.

'No, sir. She hasn't said anything like that.'

'After the money I suppose,' sniffed Leeyes.

'She's the daughter of a Mrs Erica Baskerville who herself is the daughter of Octavia Harquil-Grasset and Eric Hector Goudy of the Fearnshire Regiment . . .'

'She'll have to prove it, Sloan, that's all and . . .'

'It isn't she who's saying it, sir.'

'What? What . . .?'

'That's what Dr Dabbe says.'

'What's it got to do with him?' demanded Leeyes truculently.

'Some new test he's done, sir. It's in his report and it demonstrates the maternal inheritance of mitochondrial DNA through three generations. Jane Baskerville is Octavia Garamond's daughter's daughter . . .'

It had been Dr Dabbe who had first caught – and compared – his hairs, after all.

'These tests for DNA Mitochondrial Typing are becoming very common in the legal field, Miss Kennerley,' said James Puckle when they were next alone. 'It would have been a great help to have had them around at the time of the Tichborne claimant.'

'Jane Baskerville isn't claiming anything,' said Amelia. 'She said that she's getting married and only wanted to check on her mother's family's heredity first.'

'Very wise,' nodded James Puckle. 'I wish that more . . .'

'And that's when they found the letter in the Adoptions Register file from Great-Aunt Octavia giving her name and address in case her daughter ever consulted it.'

'I think we shall be able to tell Mrs Erica Baskerville quite a lot about her father, too,' said James Puckle, who had found out a good deal of the family history of a young Scottish officer in the Fearnshires killed in May 1940 at a place called Hautchamps.

'And about precatory settlements,' said Amelia, who also knew where her duty rested.

'And about precatory settlements,' assented the solicitor. 'When Jane's a bit stronger, though. In the mean time . . .'

'Yes?' Something in his voice made Amelia look up.

'I've booked a table for two at the White Hart . . . that is,' he said archaically, 'if you will do me the honour of joining me.'

'I can't see why all that business about cells was so important,' grumbled Crosby, always more difficult to handle when hungry.

'It's called scientific progress,' said Sloan, adding hastily, 'or would have been if the deceased hadn't decided otherwise.'

'And I still don't see how Dr Dabbe can have known about that other girl being the deceased's granddaughter without even seeing her,' persisted Crosby resentfully. 'It doesn't make sense to me.'

'That's called scientific progress too, Crosby.'

'It's all very well, sir, but how can he be so certain?'

'Don't ask me, Crosby. I don't know. You'll have to ask Dr Dabbe yourself.'

'I did, sir.' The constable still sounded aggrieved.

'And what did he say?'

'That he was as sure as eggs is eggs.'

The Catherine Aird Collection £5.99

To the outside world, Calleshire is the perfect and tranquil English county, but when you scratch beneath the surface all manner of mischief and murder reveal themselves . . .

From the pen of one of the sharpest and most ingenious contemporary crime writers come three novels featuring the inimitable talents of Detective Inspector Sloan, ably assisted by his enthusiastic, fast-driving, nonsense-talking, bad-joking constable, Crosby.

His Burial Too
Last Respects
Harm's Way

'Carefully and originally plotted, elegantly and amusingly written . . . light, ingenious and a pleasure to read' TIMES LITERARY SUPPLEMENT

'A satisfying whodunnit, gorgeously entertaining' DAILY TELEGRAPH

'Catherine Aird's delicious concoctions are never less than elegant and mischievously sharp' THE TIMES

Also available in Pan Books *The Body Politic*

All Pan books are available at your local bookshop or newsagent, or can be ordered direct from the publisher. Indicate the number of copies required and fill in the form below.

Send to: Pan C. S. Dept
             Macmillan Distribution Ltd
             Houndmills Basingstoke RG21 2XS
or phone: 0256 29242, quoting title, author and Credit Card number.

Please enclose a remittance* to the value of the cover price plus: £1.00 for the first book plus 50p per copy for each additional book ordered.

*Payment may be made in sterling by UK personal cheque, postal order, sterling draft or international money order, made payable to Pan Books Ltd.

Alternatively by Barclaycard/Access/Amex/Diners

Card No.   [ ][ ][ ][ ][ ][ ][ ][ ][ ][ ][ ][ ][ ][ ][ ][ ]

Expiry Date   [ ][ ][ ][ ][ ][ ]

_____

                    Signature:

Applicable only in the UK and BFPO addresses

While every effort is made to keep prices low, it is sometimes necessary to increase prices at short notice. Pan Books reserve the right to show on covers and charge new retail prices which may differ from those advertised in the text or elsewhere.

NAME AND ADDRESS IN BLOCK LETTERS PLEASE:

....

Name _____

Address _____

_____

_____

_____

                                                            6/92

12 76

122
150 Crosby!